I'm Not Him

I'm Not Him: The Stranger in the Mirror Was Me

Kimberly Cummings

The Cozy Scratchpad

I'm Not Him: The Stranger in the Mirror Was Me

First Edition

Printed in the United States of America

Hardcover ISBN: 979-8-9998730-2-6
Paperback ISBN: 979-8-9998730-3-3

Published by:
The Cozy Scratchpad

Disclaimer

Content Warning

This story contains themes of child loss, abduction, mental health struggles, and grief, which may be distressing to some readers. Reader discretion is advised.

Dedication

To God

Thank you for allowing me to write and share
Your holy scriptures with all readers.

Now the God of hope fill you with all joy and peace in believing, that ye may abound in hope, through the power of the Holy Ghost.

Romans 15:13 KJV

Table of Contents

Introduction

Some moments change everything.

Moments that steal the air from your lungs and shatter the ground beneath your feet. Moments when the world you knew collapses, and you're left standing in the wreckage, searching for something, anything that still feels real.

I'm Not Him is the story of one such moment. A moment that didn't just change a day, or a year, it altered lives in ways no one could have predicted.

This is a journey through the rawest corners of the human heart through identity, truth, and the kind of faith that clings on long after reason says to let go. It's about a love so fierce that it refuses to fade, even when years stretch on without answers. About the bond between parent and child, the instinct to fight for what's yours, and the courage it takes to face what you've feared most.

You'll walk through grief that settles deep into the bones. You'll sit in the silence of unanswered questions. You'll feel the weight of memories that flicker at the edge of recall, memories that demand to be faced, no matter the cost.

And through it all, you'll witness the quiet, unshakable truth: some things cannot be erased. Not by time. Not by loss. Not even by the lies that try to replace them.

This story is for every family that has waited in the dark for the sound of a loved one's footsteps. For every soul who has ever looked in the mirror and whispered: Who am I... really?

Prologue
The Loss of Jacob

The morning Jacob died was tranquil.

Emma had woken up with a strange ache in her chest, one she couldn't quite explain. The house was still wrapped in that early-morning blue, the sun not yet reaching through the thin curtains. She stretched her legs over the side of the bed and called out softly, "Jacob?" No answer. Generally, by this time, he'd be babbling from his crib, cooing and kicking his legs, ready for his morning bottle. But today there was only silence.

She walked into the nursery barefoot, her heart pounding for reasons she didn't understand. She paused at the doorway. Jacob was lying still. Too still.

"Jacob?" she whispered, moving closer. The mobile above the crib turned gently from the ceiling fan's breeze, casting shadows of stars and moons across the wall.

She reached down and touched his hand.

Cold.

Panic exploded in her chest. She shook him. Once. Twice.

"Jacob! Jacob, wake up!" she screamed, lifting him from the crib, cradling his lifeless body against her chest.

Andres burst into the room, shirt half-buttoned, his eyes widening in horror as he saw Emma collapsed on the floor, rocking back and forth with their son in her arms.

They rushed to the emergency room. The doctors moved quickly, ran tests, used machines, and whispered. Emma held

Andres's hand until it turned white from pressure. Then the final blow came, in a quiet voice and with sorrowful eyes.

"I'm so sorry. It was SIDS. Sudden Infant Death Syndrome."

There was no explanation. No warning signs. No answers. Only a finality that shattered something sacred in Emma's heart.

The funeral was a blur. Tiny white casket. White roses. Family and friends are trying not to cry too loudly. Emma felt like a ghost in her own skin.

After the service, she stopped talking for days. Wouldn't eat. Wouldn't leave the bed. She stared at the empty crib as if Jacob might still return, as if he'd been misplaced and would crawl back in when she wasn't looking.

Andres tried to comfort her, but grief had created a wall between them. Emma wasn't just mourning her child; she was mourning the person she used to be.

And deep inside, a quiet desperation began to grow, raw and dangerous, to feel whole again. To be a mother again. To fix what had been broken by death.

She didn't know then what she would become.

But something inside her had changed. Forever. And when the test on the bathroom sink showed two pink lines, Emma believed, if only for a moment, that she might have a second chance.

Chapter 1
A New Beginning

It has been two years since Jacob's passing. The test sat on the edge of the bathroom sink, still warm from her trembling hand. Two pink lines stared back at her.

Pregnant.

Emma blinked hard, as if the faint lines might shift or disappear if she stared long enough. Her throat tightened. A thousand feelings swirled inside her, bumping into each other: joy, fear, disbelief. Somewhere in the mess was a flicker of something she hadn't felt in months.

Jacob's room had been untouched since the day he was gone, a silent museum of a life that ended too soon. Most mornings, she avoided it entirely. The one time she tried to dust the shelves, she ended up curled on the floor for hours, clutching a blanket that still smelled faintly of him.

But today… something shifted.

She stepped into the living room, the test clutched like fragile evidence. She sat down slowly, eyes fixed on the tile floor, listening for Andrés' truck to pull into the driveway.

When the front door finally creaked open, the familiar scent of sweat and cardboard drifted in the smell of his long warehouse shifts. His boots thudded across the entryway. She didn't speak. She just held the test between them.

He froze mid-step. For a heartbeat, his face was unreadable. Then he crossed the room, sat beside her, and took her hand.

"You're pregnant?"

She nodded. "It's real this time. Two lines."

Andrés' thumb brushed over her knuckles. His smile was faint but steady. "Maybe… maybe this is a new beginning." As the months passed, the secret grew harder to keep.

Melissa insisted on throwing her sister a shower, even though Emma initially resisted. "It's too soon," Emma murmured, but Melissa just shook her head.

"No, you're six months pregnant. This baby deserves celebration. And so do you."

So one Saturday afternoon, the house was filled with balloons and laughter. Pastel streamers framed the doorway, a mountain of wrapped gifts sat near the couch, and Grace handed out paper cups of punch like a little hostess. Family, neighbors, and friends came bearing diapers, baby clothes, and advice.

Emma sat in the center of it all, her hands resting over her belly, smiling more than she expected to. Every so often, though, her hand would clutch the fabric of her dress a little tighter, as if she were holding the baby inside from slipping away.

Melissa leaned close at one point, whispering, "You're glowing, sis. He's going to be strong, just like you."

Emma's eyes stung, but she nodded. "I want to believe that."

When it was Grace's turn to give her gift, she held out a stuffed giraffe nearly as big as she was. "For him," she said proudly. Emma hugged her niece, blinking back tears. She smiled, but her eyes burned. "Thank you, Gracie. He'll love it."

Everyone laughed and passed around cake, and the house filled with chatter. Andrés stayed close, his arm brushing hers, whispering whenever her smile faltered. It's okay. Breathe. We're here.

For a few hours, Emma let herself believe it. That joy was possible again, that this baby might be her second chance.

Three months later, under the dim lights of Merry Hospital, Carlos Michael Díaz came into the world wailing. Black hair matted against his head, eyes tightly shut, his cry filled the delivery room like a declaration. Emma laughed through her tears, clutching him to her chest as if her heartbeat alone could keep him alive.

Andrés hovered close, one hand on her shoulder, the other brushing over the baby's tiny fingers. "He's perfect," he whispered. Grace, only eight years old at the time, tiptoed into the hospital room later with her mother, Melissa, clutching the same stuffed giraffe. She peered over the edge of the bed, eyes wide. "He's so small," she whispered. Emma guided her closer, letting her stroke Carlos's hand.

The first weeks were a blur of midnight feedings, sponge baths, and the soft, sweet smell of new life. Andrés would sometimes catch Emma just watching Carlos sleep, her hand resting gently on his chest, feeling the rise and fall. But even in the gentle rhythm of new parenthood, there were cracks barely noticeable at first. Emma rarely let anyone else hold him. If Andrés took Carlos to give her a break, she hovered nearby, offering corrections. Grace noticed, but she didn't have the words for it yet.

One evening, after Andrés had finally coaxed Carlos into a peaceful sleep, Emma stood at the doorway of the nursery, one hand on the frame. Her voice was soft but certain. "I'm not losing him. Not him."

Chapter 2
The Happy Years

The Díaz home changed overnight. Bottles lined the counter, the scent of baby powder clung to the air, and a soft bassinet sat beside their bed. Carlos's cries split the night every few hours, sending Emma from her pillow to his side in a heartbeat.

Sometimes Andrés tried to help, scooping Carlos up while fumbling with a bottle, but Emma would hover, whispering corrections until he handed the baby back. He didn't argue. He understood.

There were sweet moments, too. Naps on Andrés' chest, his tiny body rising and falling with each breath. And visits from family, Melissa dropping by with casseroles, Grace kneeling by the bassinet to sing lullabies, neighbors stopping with flowers. The house, once so heavy with silence, now pulsed with life.

Emma often found herself simply watching Carlos sleep, one hand pressed lightly against his chest to feel the steady rhythm. She prayed quietly each time. Please don't take him from me. Not this one.

It became the anchor that shaped her days. With Carlos in her arms, life slowly softened. She still hovered, still worried at every cough and restless night, but the sharp edge of grief dulled under the sound of his laughter. For the first time in two years, their home held music again.

Summer arrived with vast skies and a promise of freedom. One Saturday, Andrés carried Carlos in his arms as they strolled through the park, while Emma found a quiet spot beneath a great oak. She spread a blanket in the shade, then took Carlos gently from Andrés. Cradling him in her lap, Emma breathed in his hair; it smelled of sunshine and fresh grass. They lingered there for hours, sharing sandwiches and cookies, and Emma thought, "Maybe joy really can last."

Nights were just as precious. After long warehouse shifts, Andrés would come home, flip on the radio, and sweep Emma into the kitchen. "Dance with me," he'd whisper, spinning her slowly until their laughter woke Carlos from his crib. Those were the nights when Emma dared to dream again. In the weeks that followed, joy lingered in the small moments at home, too.

Now four months old, Carlos lay on a blanket near the window, kicking his legs wildly. When Andrés leaned down and made a silly face, a bubble of laughter escaped Carlos' lips. He reached out with clumsy fists, batting at the toy hanging above him. Emma pressed her hand over her mouth, eyes shining, as her baby boy found his voice, and his joy filled the quiet house.

Then, one morning, Emma stood in the bathroom again. Another test. Another two pink lines. Her hands trembled, her heart pounding with both hope and terror.

When she told Andrés, he pulled her into his arms, whispering against her hair, "We've been given another blessing."

Nine months later, under the sterile hospital lights, Benjamin Isaiah Diaz entered the world with a cry so fierce it startled Emma into laughter. Tears streaked her cheeks as she pressed him to her chest. "Two," she whispered. "God gave us two."

Andrés kissed her damp forehead. "Two blessings. Two promises."

With Ben's arrival, their home swelled with new rhythms. Carlos, 13 months old, peeked into the crib with wide eyes, whispering secrets to his baby brother. Emma caught him one afternoon, laying his favorite toy truck beside Ben's blanket. Carlos hugged the toy to his chest, then looked at his brother with wide eyes.

"Mine," he said firmly. He paused, thinking hard, then held it out.

Seasons turned, and their house filled with small adventures. Rainy days became forts of blankets and pillows. Andrés strung Christmas lights inside while Carlos toddled across the cushions, giggling as he plopped down. From Emma's arms, newborn Ben made soft little noises, his tiny fists waving at the glow of the lights. Emma's laughter spilled into the small room, warm and unguarded. She bent her head, whispering into Ben's tiny ear, "See your brother? That's Carlos."

When winter came, Andrés stepped into the snowy yard with Carlos bundled in layers. He let himself fall backward into a drift with a loud "oof!" Carlos squealed, wobbling on his chubby legs. He bent down, scooped a mitten full of snow, and tossed it just far enough to sprinkle Andrés' coat. Emma watched from the porch, rocking Ben close against her chest, the baby's eyes fluttering in the bright winter light. She kissed the top of his head and murmured, "One day, you'll be out there too." Emma stood on the porch a few minutes longer with Ben bundled in her arms, her cheeks pink from the cold, her heart swelling at the sight of her son tumbling joyfully in the snow, then she retreated inside their home. Spring blossomed with Easter mornings. Emma buttoned Carlos's shirt while Andrés dressed Ben in infant-sized suspenders. In church, hymns filled the sanctuary, and Emma reached for Andrés's hand, whispering, "I never thought I'd feel whole again." His reply was steady: "This is our miracle, Emma. Don't ever forget."

Summer nights smelled of grilled corn and smoky charcoal. Andrés flipped burgers while Carlos darted through the sprinkler and Ben babbled from his blanket. Later, marshmallows roasted over glowing coals, Carlos smeared with chocolate, Ben asleep in Andrés's lap. "Promise me," Andrés whispered, his eyes on the firelight, "we'll give them this kind of happiness forever."

Emma pressed her first finger to his lips, voice thick. "I promise."

It was a joyful year. Their laughter filled every corner, their children's footsteps marking the days with innocence. To anyone else, the Díaz family looked untouchable, wrapped in light.

But in Emma's heart, a shadow lingered. Each night as she tucked her sons into bed, she whispered silent prayers, her hand trembling against the doorframe. She couldn't shake the fear that joy was fragile, that it could all vanish in a single breath.

She stood one evening in the nursery doorway, Ben asleep in his crib, Carlos's laughter still echoing faintly from the other room. Her voice was soft, certain, and edged with fear.

Chapter 3
Anchored in Love

The Diaz's home was no longer quiet. Two little boys filled every corner with noise, pattering footsteps, high-pitched giggles, and the endless chatter of make-believe games. Emma would sometimes pause in the middle of folding laundry or stirring a pot on the stove, closing her eyes to listen. It was music, a symphony of life she thought she had lost forever. Carlos had naturally taken to the role of big brother. At four, he considered himself Ben's teacher, protector, and sometimes his boss, whether Ben liked it or not. Emma often caught him kneeling beside his toddler bed, speaking in a slow, exaggerated voice.

"Say 'car,' Benny. Car. Like mine."

Ben would blink, then he would say, "car, before bursting into laughter that sent Carlos into fits of giggles.

Andrés would lean against the doorframe, arms folded, shaking his head. "He's teaching him to drive before he can sprint."

Emma smiled, her heart swelling at the sight. "Better that than fighting already."

Grace came over often with Melissa. She was twelve now, with the air of someone who considered herself practically grown. She adored the boys, doting on them as though they were her dolls.

One afternoon, while Emma and Melissa sat on the porch drinking iced tea, Grace spread a blanket in the yard and placed Ben in the middle. She handed him blocks and showed him how to stack them.

"Here, Benny, like this." She guided his small hands. When he knocked them over, she laughed and hugged him tight. "Don't worry, I'll always look out for you."

Emma overheard the words, her throat tightening. She looked at Melissa, who was watching her daughter with pride.

"She's got your heart," Emma whispered.

Melissa reached over and squeezed her hand. "And you've got your smile back."

That weekend, Melissa insisted on another family picnic at the park. She spread out a blanket beneath a wide oak tree, her laughter carrying across the grass as the children ran in circles.

Carlos chased butterflies, shrieking with joy, while Grace twirled around him in mock competition. Ben ran after them, short legs pumping with determination. When he tripped on the uneven grass, Andrés swooped in, scooping him up and swinging him high into the air until his laughter rang out like bells. Melissa shook her head, grinning. "Look at you, Emma. A few years ago, you were shattered. Now…" She gestured toward the children, toward Andrés tossing Ben into the air, toward Emma's smile. "Now you're glowing again."

Emma's eyes misted. "I just want to hold onto it forever. That's all I ask."

Melissa's smile softened, but her voice carried the weight of truth. "Then keep holding on. These are the days you'll remember when the storms come."

Back at home, Carlos loved showing off his "skills." He stacked blocks for Ben, taught him how to kick a ball across the yard, and even tried to read him bedtime stories. One night,

Emma peeked into the boys' room and found Carlos sitting cross-legged on the floor with a picture book spread wide.

"This is a dog," Carlos explained carefully, pointing. "Woof, woof. Say it, Benny."

Ben said it just as he was told to do, and Carlos cheered as if he had scored a goal. "See, Mamá? He's learning!"

Emma's laughter filled the doorway. "He's got the best teacher."

Carlos puffed his chest proudly. "He'll always have me."

On Sundays, they would dress in their finest clothes and walk together to church. Emma loved the way people's faces lit up at the sight of her boys. "They're getting so big," the older women in the congregation would say, and Emma's heart swelled with pride.

That Easter, the sanctuary bloomed with lilies. Emma buttoned Carlos's shirt, smoothed Ben's tiny suspenders, and clasped Andrés's hand as they sang together. For a moment, with hymns rising and sunlight streaming through stained glass, Emma felt whole.

After the church service, the children scattered across the churchyard for an egg hunt. Emma leaned into Andrés, whispering, "This is what happiness looks like."

He kissed her temple. "And it's ours."

That summer, the town parade brought music and laughter. Clowns tossed candy, floats glittered, and marching bands rattled the pavement. Carlos darted forward to scoop up candy, while Ben sat proudly on Andrés's shoulders, clapping in time with the drums.

Confetti swirled, children screamed with delight, and Emma laughed until her cheeks ached. For that day, worries faded into the background.

When the children were finally asleep, Emma and Andrés often sat together on the porch. The cicadas hummed in the trees, fireflies blinking across the yard. Andrés leaned back, sipping lemonade.

"We've built something good here, haven't we?" he asked softly.

Emma rested her head on his shoulder. "Yes. But sometimes it feels too good, like it can't last."

He tightened his arm around her. "It will. We'll make sure it does."

She wanted to believe him. She wanted to let his certainty drown out her fear. Yet when she rose later to check the boys, she lingered in the doorway, her hand trembling on the frame.

Ben was still awake and darted across the rug, tumbling into Carlos's arms. The two boys rolled together in a heap of laughter, their giggles bouncing through the room. Emma clapped, tears stinging her eyes as she scooped them close, their warm little bodies pressed against her.

"Now get back in bed, you two," she said softly.

That night, long after Andrés had drifted to sleep, she woke to faint noises from the boys' room. Peeking in, she found Ben murmuring soft words in his dreams, clutching his blanket, while Carlos stirred restlessly in his bed.

Emma whispered into the shadows, her voice both a prayer and a promise.

"You're my whole world. Both of you. I won't let anything take you from me."

She believed it then with all her heart, clinging to the hope that love alone could hold them safe forever.

Chapter 4
The Quiet Before the Spiral

Five years had passed since Emma first held Carlos in her arms, whispering promises only a mother could make. Now five years old, he carried the boundless energy of a boy who leapt before he looked. Four years had passed since Ben's arrival, her second gift, now a thoughtful four-year-old who trailed his big brother like a shadow.

The house had grown louder with each passing year. Carlos had a streak of energy that made him fearless, running, climbing, and leaping without thinking twice. Ben was quieter but adored his big brother, trailing after him like a shadow. Together, they filled every room with noise, laughter, and the occasional squabble.

That morning, Emma buckled the boys into their seats, tugging each strap twice the way she always did.

"List?" Carlos asked, swinging his legs.

"In my head," she said, tapping her temple. "Bananas, milk, eggs, bread, and...?"

"Cereal with the tiger," he announced.

Ben chimed in from the other side, "Sprinkles!"

"Not a food group," Emma said, smiling despite herself. "We'll see."

The store doors sighed open, and a wash of cool air met them. Ben reached up for the cart handle.

"I push?"

"You can help," Emma said, placing his small hands on the bar while she steered. Carlos jogged a step ahead, then remembered and came back to walk beside them, hopping from tile to tile.

In produce, Ben held each apple like a treasure, placing them into a bag with exaggerated care and a little grunt after every drop.

"Gentle," Emma murmured. "They bruise."

Carlos pointed at the bananas. "We need the big bunch. I'm strong now."

"You were strong yesterday," Emma teased. "We'll take this one, and you can carry it to the belt."

By the time they reached the cereal aisle, Carlos's eyes had gone bright. He pressed his palms to the box with the cartoon tiger as if it might run away.

"Please?"

Emma looked from the box to his face. He was five, but sometimes that particular tilt of his mouth made him look two again. "One box," she said. "And no opening it in the car."

He nodded solemnly, as if she'd sworn him into office.

At checkout, Emma slid items onto the belt while the boys "helped." Carlos hoisted the bananas like a trophy. Ben counted the apples, skipping numbers and giggling each time he realized it.

"Eight... nine... eleven!"

"Close enough," Emma said, handing them each a receipt to "guard" for the walk to the car.

On the drive home, the afternoon hung warm and bright. The little ice cream shop with the striped awning appeared on the corner, and the decision was made before Emma finished thinking about it.

"Ice cream?" she asked.

"Ice cream!" both boys cried.

They ate on the bench out front, the world slowed to drips and licks. Carlos chose chocolate and committed fully chin, cheeks, and one eyebrow. Ben's cone wore a confetti of rainbow sprinkles that slid down his fingers in sticky trails.

"Napkins," Emma said, handing them a stack they barely used. She watched their mouths go busy, and their eyes go soft, that small contentment she wished she could bottle.

"This is the best day," Ben declared, spraying sprinkles as he spoke.

"Best day," Carlos echoed through chocolate teeth, and Emma laughed because they were right.

Back home, the yard beckoned. Carlos kicked off his shoes and sprinted through the grass, a blur of knees and elbows. Ben followed, determined to keep up, his laughter bobbing behind him like a kite tail.

"Shoes!" Emma called, holding them up.

"Just five minutes?" Carlos pleaded, already halfway to the patch of clover.

Emma glanced at the laundry basket she'd left by the door, then at their faces. "Five," she said, and the five grew the way summer minutes do.

They turned sticks into swords, then into fishing poles, without moving an inch. Carlos invented a game in which the square of shade beneath the maple was "lava," and the sunlit grass was an island. Ben tried to copy his brother's leaps, arms windmilling, landing with a thud and a crow.

"Careful," Emma called, but her voice had no edge. She was barefoot now, too, toes greened by grass, a habit she'd drifted away from until today.

A robin hopped close and then away, and Ben froze, whispering, "Shh," as if he could coax it into friendship. Carlos dug his fingers into the dirt and found a worm.

"Look!" he shouted, holding it up like a ribbon.

Emma winced and then didn't. "We put him back where he belongs," she said, and watched Carlos kneel and return the little life to its cool tunnel, proud of the gentleness he showed when he remembered to.

They chased a soccer ball until it lodged under the lilac bush and then became a treasure to be rescued. Dust streaked Carlos's shins. Ben's palms went brown to the heel. The knees of their pants told a story in smears.

"Andrés will faint when he sees this laundry," Emma said to no one, and everyone, because saying his name out loud made the day feel anchored.

By late afternoon, the sun had shifted and the shade stretched long, the kind of light that makes you think about dinner without moving toward it. Emma clapped her hands.

"Inside. Mud parade is over."

Groans, bargaining, then the shuffle of surrender: a line of small, dirty feet up the back steps.

In the bathroom, she turned the faucet until the water ran warm and steady. Steam ghosted the mirror. Ben's fingerprints appeared and vanished as he traced circles on the glass.

"Your turn first, sticky man."

"I'm not sticky," he protested, climbing into the tub with a squeak and a splash that proved otherwise.

She soaped his arms, his neck, the little dirt crescents tucked beneath each nail. He made a fleet of bubbles in his palms and blew them away with an enormous puff.

"Magic," Ben whispered, delighted.

"Don't teach your brother spells," Emma said softly.

From the doorway, Carlos drove two toy cars along the tile, narrating their races with the breathless commentary of a tiny sports announcer.

"Can I do the hair swish?" Ben asked, his little fingers already gripping the tub's rim.

"One hair swish," Emma allowed, smiling despite herself. He dunked under, came up grinning, water streaming down his cheeks like silver threads.

Emma laughed softly, reaching for a towel but setting it aside for later. He wasn't done yet, and she loved the sight of his joy too much to end it.

"You look like a burrito," Carlos piped up with a grin, cars clutched in his hands.

"I'm a dragon burrito," Ben corrected proudly.

"Rawr," Emma added, baring her teeth just enough to make them both dissolve into laughter that echoed down the hall.

For one fleeting second, it felt like everything was normal again. No cries. No shadows. Just two boys, their laughter filling the walls.

"Carlos, go play in the hallway while I finish Ben's bath," Emma said gently.

He groaned, dragging his feet, but obeyed. His cars scraped along the wall as he stomped toward the banister, narrating their race in a breathless announcer's voice.

Steam ghosted across the mirror, curling into soft clouds, and the smell of shampoo mixed with warm water wrapped the bathroom in a cocoon. Emma leaned over Ben, rinsing suds from his curls. She laid a towel on the counter, then stepped into the hallway closet for another.

Behind her, the house answered back Carlos's wheels rattling against the upstairs railing, Ben's humming as he patted the porcelain rim, the ordinary chorus of home. Safe sounds. Familiar sounds.

She was halfway back to the bathroom when it happened.

A sharp, hollow thud cracked through the air like the snap of a branch in winter.

Emma froze, her heart in her throat. Then another sound: the short, startled cry of a child, cut off too quickly.

Carlos.

She gripped the towel and sprinted toward the landing.

Later, she would wonder what he had been thinking, whether he genuinely believed he could leap and land on his feet like one of the superheroes on his bedroom posters, or if it was just the wild impulse of a boy lost in his own game. She would never know.

All she saw was the aftermath.

Carlos lay crumpled at the bottom of the stairs, toy cars scattered across the floor like broken teeth. One wheel still spun in a slow, lopsided circle before toppling. His limbs bent wrong, his face turned toward her, eyes half-closed.

"Carlos?" Her voice cracked, thin as paper.

The word caught in her throat as the towel slipped from her arms. She stumbled down the steps, knees nearly giving way, and dropped beside him.

"Baby!" Her cry tore from somewhere deeper than breath as she scooped him into her arms. His body was limp, heavier than she remembered. She sank to the floor, rocking him, whispering his name over and over as her pulse thundered in her ears.

Time fractured. She couldn't tell if it was minutes or only seconds. All she knew was Carlos's stillness, the weight of him pressing against her chest.

And then...

Ben.

Her stomach dropped. She bolted to her feet, laying Carlos carefully on the rug, and tore back up the stairs, socks slipping on the hardwood.

The bathroom door banged open. Ben floated motionless near the edge, curls plastered to his forehead, lips pale as porcelain.

Emma's scream was raw, animal, unrecognizable. "No, no, no, no, no."

She lunged for the tub, her hands shaking as she pulled Ben's small body from the water. He was limp, slick, and terrifyingly silent. Water streamed down her robe as she collapsed onto the tile, clutching him against her chest.

Blood streaked down from a gash on his forehead where he must have struck the porcelain rim in his frantic scramble to follow her. The crimson mingled with the water, turning her lap into a spreading stain of red and clear.

"Ben, baby, breathe, please, please." Her words dissolved into sobs. She rocked him, pressing trembling kisses into his wet curls, whispering his name between gasps.

But his lips were pale, his lashes clumped, his chest unmoving.

She couldn't remember how long she had been downstairs.

A minute? Five? Ten?

Time had collapsed into a blur the moment Carlos fell. In the haze of screams and pounding blood in her ears, the house had become a battlefield of silence and noise.

Had she heard splashes? The frantic gurgle of water as Ben struggled? Or had he been knocked unconscious the instant his head struck the porcelain, slipping quietly beneath the surface while she clutched his brother downstairs?

She didn't know. She would never know.

It didn't matter.

By the time she remembered, by the time she rushed back upstairs, it was already too late.

In the space of one ordinary evening, both of her boys were gone. And the house, once filled with noise, fell into a silence that would never leave her.

Downstairs, Carlos still lay where she had left him, his small body twisted and still, toy cars scattered like forgotten relics around him.

That day shattered her completely. Her mind, already fragile from grief, splintered beyond repair. She could not hold the weight of it, could not piece together how one ordinary evening had collapsed into ruin.

She would never tell anyone the whole truth about Ben, not then. Not right away. Some parts were too jagged, too unspeakable, to let out into the world.

But in the space of minutes, she had lost both of her boys.

The laughter, the footsteps, the safe hum of a house alive with children, gone.

And the world, once noisy and full, fell silent.

Chapter 5
The Disappearance

Later that evening, Emma sat on the worn rug in the upstairs hallway, her back pressed against the wall outside the children's room. Around her, piles of toddler shirts and footed pajamas lay scattered, their fabric limp and faded, stripped of the warm scent of her boys. Her eyes were bloodshot, her lips cracked from dehydration. The air felt heavy, almost suffocating, as if mildew clung to it, laced with something else, something darker.

Jacob was gone. Carlos was gone. Ben was gone. She mouthed the words silently, but never dared say them out loud.

The washing machine still held their last small outfits, damp and cold. She hadn't been able to touch them. It was as if time itself had frozen at the moment her life shattered.

One moment, Carlos's voice was in the hallway, laughter spilling into the bathroom. Next, she was cradling him at the foot of the stairs, broken and still.

And in the chaos, she had forgotten that Ben was still in the tub.

The memory clawed its way back in fragments: the slap of tiny hands against porcelain, the frantic scrape of fingernails, the dull crack of his head striking the rim, and the soft, terrible gurgle of water.

Emma pressed her palms hard against her ears, but the sounds wouldn't leave her. They never would.

Her body rocked slowly, without rhythm, her gaze fixed on nothing. The pale evening light coming through the curtains seemed too bright, slicing the room into harsh strips of shadow.

Suddenly, amid her daze, she heard the front door creak open downstairs. She didn't move. Heavy footsteps moved across the hardwood. A pause. Then the sound of something dropping, a bag?, and silence.

When Andrés stepped into the hallway, his gaze caught instantly on the blood smeared along the floor near the stairs. His pulse kicked hard.

"Emma?" he called, his voice rough. No answer.

He took the stairs two at a time, his boots sticking to the tacky smear of drying blood on the landing. He rounded the corner...

And stopped.

Emma sat slumped against the wall, her hair tangled and damp, eyes vacant. In her lap, she cradled Ben, rocking him gently as if he were only asleep, whispering words Andrés couldn't hear. He noticed a dark stain on Ben's forehead.

Just beyond her, Carlos lay sprawled on the floor, his leg twisted unnaturally, his skin pale, his lips faintly blue.

Andrés's breath caught. For a moment, the hallway tilted. He couldn't move. Couldn't breathe. His family, his boys, were scattered before him, broken in ways he couldn't yet understand.

Seconds passed, stretching into what felt like minutes. The house was silent except for the faint hum of the refrigerator downstairs, so ordinary against the horror in front of him.

Then Emma's voice broke the stillness.

"They're not dead," she whispered, eyes glazed and far away. "They're just sleeping."

Andres' breath hitched. He knelt beside Carlos and lifted him into his arms. The boy's body was limp, unnaturally heavy, his head lolling against Andres' shoulder. A faint coldness seeped through the fabric of Andres' shirt.

"What did you do?" His voice broke in the middle, shattering under the weight of grief as tears streamed down his cheeks.

Emma didn't look at him. Her gaze stayed somewhere far away, her fingers stroking Ben's hair in slow, mechanical motions.

Andrés rose unsteadily and stepped toward the bathroom. The tub still brimmed with water, its surface tinged a faint reddish haze from Ben's blood. The sight was chaos: towels strewn across the floor, water dripping in slow trails down the tiles, the sharp tang of iron thick in the air.

His chest burned. Anger coiled tight inside him, swelling with each breath until it pressed against his ribs. Grief tangled with frustration, leaving his hands trembling at his sides.

"Why didn't you call for help?" he shouted, his voice raw, ragged with disbelief.

Emma froze. Slowly, she turned her head, her eyes drifting past Andrés to the limp body in his arms. When she finally spoke, her voice was flat, drained of all feeling.

"We need to leave."

The words hit him like a slap. "Leave?"

"Now."

Something in her tone, calm, certain, unnerved him more than the blood on the floor.

Later that night, under a heavy moon, they carried Carlos outside. Andrés's arms ached from the weight, but it wasn't the muscles straining. It was something deeper, heavier, a weight pressing against his soul.

They placed the boy near the trash cans behind the house, the smell of blood mingling with the damp earth and sour rot of old garbage.

"He's better off," Emma murmured, almost to herself, eyes fixed on nothing.

Andrés's stomach lurched. He staggered to the side of the house, bracing one hand against the cold siding as bile surged up his throat. He vomited into the shadows, his body heaving, tears stinging his eyes. Each convulsion felt like it tore something inside him, something that would never be whole again.

When the sickness finally passed, he wiped his mouth with the back of his sleeve, chest burning. He glanced back at Emma, still standing motionless, still detached, as if she were carved from stone.

The sight chilled him more than the night air.

He walked to the SUV. His hands moved automatically, loading bags into the back. He helped Emma into the passenger seat.

He did not ask questions.

He just drove.

They drove through the night, ending up in a cheap motel on the far edge of New Jersey. Emma sat by the window, her breath fogging the glass, mumbling in broken fragments.

"He's still here. I can hear him… Jacob's crying…"

After a couple of days, Andrés was still drifting from place to place, renting rooms in different motels across the city. He paid in cash, gave names that weren't his, and moved on before anyone could notice. None of it felt real, like he was floating outside his own body.

At night, Emma rocked herself in the corner, humming lullabies to no one. The shadows on the walls became ghosts. The mirrors whispered names.

Jacob. Carlos. Ben.

She saw them in every reflection.

Andres lay on the stiff motel bed, staring at the ceiling. The heater's hum was too loud. His chest felt heavy.

He told himself he'd done the right thing, protecting Emma, sparing her the pain of prison. But the images wouldn't stop: Carlos' head limp against his shoulder, Ben's still hair dripping onto Emma's lap.

He swallowed hard, trying to push the thoughts down. But they rose again, sharper this time, wrapping around his ribs.

He'd let them die in silence.

And he wasn't sure if that was for her… or himself.

After a week, Andres returned to work, pretending his life hadn't been burned to the ground. He worked in the warehouse by day and held his wife while she unraveled by night. He didn't tell anyone the truth. Not even himself.

But at night, when Emma's breathing was steady beside him, he lay awake staring at the motel ceiling. The hum of the heater became the gurgle of bathwater. The faint drip in the bathroom sink became the sound of Carlos's head hitting the stairs.

Every morning, he buried it again, deeper than the day before.

It never stayed buried for long.

Then, one morning, Emma disappeared.

It was a Tuesday.

Emma had been silent all morning, watching the news on the motel TV while eating dry Cheerios with her fingers. Suddenly, she stood up, brushed her hair, and said, "I need to go for a walk."

Andres didn't question it. He needed air, too. And maybe, if he didn't follow her, he wouldn't have to wonder what she was thinking. Perhaps he could pretend just a little longer.

Emma took the bus to the mall. Before entering, she tucked her hair inside a black baseball cap and slipped on dark glasses.

She wandered the children's section of a department store, her fingers grazing the sleeves of tiny jackets. She hummed a lullaby under her breath, her eyes glassy, distant. No one seemed to notice. Shoppers moved around her in a tide of indifference, unaware of the storm standing between racks of winter coats.

Then she saw him.

A little boy, about four years old, with a mop of dark curls and a gap-toothed smile, sat in the corner of the mall's play area. He was making the stuffed tiger roar in tiny growls, oblivious to the chatter and foot traffic around him.

Emma stood just outside the entrance, her hands tucked into the sleeves of her sweater, watching.

The boy's mother knelt to tie her shoelace, glancing up at him every few seconds. Her purse sat open on the bench, a ring of house keys glinting in the light. She told herself she was only looking away for a moment, just long enough to fix the knot in her shoe, before they went to get pretzels.

Emma waited, her gaze locked on the boy with the toy tiger clutched in his hands. The mall's hum faded until all she heard was the squeak with every squeeze.

She crouched beside him, her smile gentle, practiced.

"That's a brave tiger," she whispered. "I have one at home just like it. Do you want to see?"

The boy's eyes lit with curiosity.

Behind them, his mother tugged at her shoelace, distracted, unaware.

"Come on, baby. Let's go home."

The boy looked at her with wide, trusting eyes. He rose without question, clutching the tiger, and slipped his small hand into hers.

From the bench, the mother thumbed through a crumpled flyer from the toy store, smiling faintly at the sale circled in red. She tucked it back into her purse, digging for her wallet, then glanced up once, twice, and froze.

"Elijah?"

41

Her voice sharpened as her head whipped side to side. The spot where her son had been only moments ago was now empty.

Her voice was too soft at first. Too late.

By the time she stood, her heart slamming in her chest, they were already gone, swallowed into the shifting tide of shoppers.

Emma brought him back to the motel, her eyes bright with fevered joy.

"Ben," she said, as if the name alone could erase the truth. "It's a miracle. Our child came back to us."

Andres stared at the boy, at the unfamiliar eyes, the wrong hair, the subtle difference in his smile. His throat tightened, his chest constricted, but he forced the words out.

"Okay."

Emma didn't notice. She was already dressing Elijah in Ben's old clothes, feeding him Ben's favorite snacks, and reading from Ben's books.

When she rocked him to sleep that night, she whispered into his curls, "You're back. Mommy's so happy you found your way home."

Meanwhile...

Across town, a woman collapsed to the floor, screaming her son's name. The sound tore through the crowded mall, echoing over the chaos. Police swarmed the scene, their radios crackling with urgency. Security footage, hurriedly replayed in the control room, showed a grainy image of a woman gripping Elijah's hand and leading him away, her face just out of focus.

Andres and Emma fled again.

By the time they reached New York from New Jersey, they had dyed the boy's hair and given him a new name. Emma kept Ben Diaz's Social Security card and birth certificate readily available in case anyone inquired about Elijah.

She taught him to say, "I've always been with Mommy."

And when he got confused, when he asked about his other mom, Emma would cup his cheeks and say, "That was just a dream, sweetheart. You're mine. You've always been mine."

And slowly, a year later, Elijah forgot.

Somewhere in the shadows of their past, another story waited, one they refused to speak of, one they would never dare to face.

Andrés and Emma never looked back.

One day, they would have to.

Chapter 6
The Night I Listened

Grace sat silently at the bottom of the staircase, legs tucked beneath her, a notebook resting against her knees.

The house was still except for the low hum of the refrigerator and the occasional groan of old pipes. It was far too late for her to be awake, but something in her chest wouldn't let her sleep.

She had heard the door open a soft click, followed by footsteps. Familiar ones. Her mother. And... Aunt Emma?

Grace froze. It had been nearly six months since she'd last seen Aunt Emma. She'd stopped going over there, something about the way Aunt Emma would watch her while she played with Carlos and Ben, eyes never blinking, lips moving in strange murmurs, had left her uneasy. Now, from the steps, she stayed still, listening.

The voices came from the living room. Emma's was taut, like a stretched wire ready to snap. Her mother was careful, almost tiptoeing through each sentence.

"I don't know how to go on," Emma said. Her voice cracked, sending a pang through Grace's chest. "Every time I close my eyes, I see his face. Every time I breathe, I feel like I'm stealing air he deserved."

"You're grieving," Melissa murmured. "That's normal, Emma. You went through something no one should have to..."

"No." The word cut sharply. "You don't get it. This isn't grief. I feel like I'm unraveling. Like the real me died with him."

The room went still. Grace pressed herself against the banister.

"I still hear him," Emma whispered. "I talk to him sometimes. I used to go into his room and reach for him. But it's all gone.

"You still have Carlos and Ben," Melissa offered gently. "They need you. You were just happy. What happened?"

Silence. Then Emma's voice, colder: "I don't... want to talk about them."

"But they're your boys."

"No. They were." A pause. "But now..." She stopped herself.

Grace's pencil slipped slightly in her fingers.

"You need to talk to someone," Melissa tried again. "A counselor. Someone who can help you work through this."

"I'm not insane," Emma snapped.

"I didn't say you were..."

"Then stop treating me like I'm crazy!"

Melissa's voice lowered. "You're scaring me."

Emma gave a short, humorless laugh. "Do you know what it's like to look in the mirror and not recognize your own eyes?"

The following words came quieter, steady in a way that made Grace's stomach knot.

"I had a dream. A little boy. Not Jacob, but like him. He smiled at me. Reached for me. I could feel his arms around my neck. He was warm. Real. Alive."

Melissa stayed quiet. Grace could almost see her mother's worried expression.

"I think God is giving me a second chance," Emma went on. "Another child. One who needs me. One who will love me the way Jacob did."

"You can't replace Jacob," Melissa said. "You have Carlos and Ben…"

Emma's voice dropped to a whisper. "They're not here anymore."

"What do you mean?"

"I don't want to talk about it."

"Emma…"

"I said I don't want to talk about it!"

The air in the hallway seemed to thicken.

Melissa's tone was careful. "You don't have to talk. But I need you to listen. This… this isn't how you heal."

"I know what I saw. I know what I felt. God led me to him. I found him. And now I feel whole again."

Melissa's voice sharpened. "What did you do?"

"I gave a child love," Emma said with unsettling calm. "That's all. I gave him what no one else could. A mother."

From the stairwell, Grace's pulse pounded in her ears. She didn't understand all the words, but the wrongness in them pressed heavily on her.

Pencil dropped.

She slowly picked it up, trying not to make a sound.

Then Emma said something that froze her blood.

"I know she's listening. Your daughter. Grace. She hears everything."

Grace's breath caught.

"She's just a kid," Melissa said uneasily.

"She needs to understand," Emma murmured. "What it's like to lose a part of yourself. To know pain that claws into your chest and doesn't let go."

"She's a good girl," Melissa said softly. "And she's scared. We all are."

There was a pause. Footsteps. A door closing. Silence.

Grace stayed in the shadows for a long time, notebook clutched to her chest. Finally, with shaking hands, she opened it and wrote:

Aunt Emma said God gave her another child.

But she didn't say where he came from.

She didn't mention Carlos. Or Ben.

Emma's voice from moments before still echoed in her ears: I need to leave now. I have approximately a 50-minute drive home.

Wait. What?

"When did you move?" her mother had asked.

Emma hadn't answered.

Grace didn't know what Emma was hiding. But she knew it was something dark.

She never told anyone about that night.

She hugged the notebook to her chest and stayed on the stairs until her legs went numb, trying to convince herself she'd only imagined it.

Only then did the memory slam back into her, her aunt's voice, low and strange, slipping into something unrecognizable.

That night, Grace listened.

Far from the shadows of that night, another family in New York was living a moment they thought would last forever.

A Memory Before the Party

Two months later, Matthew Colon was turning four. The apartment was quiet except for the flicker of a late-night comedy show on TV, its laughter barely noticed. Javier and Elena sat cross-legged on the living room floor, surrounded by scraps of bright wrapping paper, half-inflated balloons, and the warm scent of vanilla cupcakes still cooling in the kitchen.

Javier tied the final bow on a large box containing Matthew's new red big-wheel Truck. He gave it a pat, a smile tugging at his lips.

"Four years old," he murmured, glancing at Elena as she filled goodie bags. "Where did the time go?"

Elena chuckled, brushing a strand of hair from her face. "I swear I blinked, and now he's riding circles around the parking lot like he's training for a professional racecar tournament."

Javier leaned back against the couch, fatigue settling in as the lamplight cast warm shadows across the room.

"Do you remember the day he was born?" he asked suddenly.

Her smile softened. "Like it was yesterday."

It had been a sweltering July afternoon, the kind that made the city feel alive with sirens and heat. Elena was folding laundry when the first pain struck a deep, tightening wave that made her drop a onesie and grip the kitchen counter.

By the time Javier rushed her to the hospital, her contractions were five minutes apart. She clung to the dashboard as if it were the only thing keeping her grounded.

"It's happening," Javier had said, his voice shaking almost as much as her hands.

In the hospital, time blurred. Nurses moved in and out like shadows. Elena pushed through the pain, her only thought to bring him into the world.

And then, a cry. Loud. Strong. Beautiful.

Tiny, red-faced, wrapped in a hospital blanket, he was placed in her arms. Tears streaked her cheeks as she kissed his damp forehead.

"Matthew," she whispered. "My sweet boy."

Javier stood beside her, speechless, his hand trembling as he touched his son's tiny fingers.

Back in the present, Elena smiled faintly. "He still looks like you. But he's got my stubborn streak."

Javier laughed softly and pulled her close. For a moment, they just sat together, surrounded by ribbons and toys, holding on to the joy of tomorrow.

"I hope he remembers these days," Elena murmured. "The good ones. The love."

"He will," Javier said. "Even if he doesn't remember the details, he'll remember how it felt."

The truck sat ready beside the couch, battery charged. Tomorrow, Matthew would race down the parking lot, grinning ear to ear.

Javier reached for Elena's hand and gave it a gentle squeeze. "He's going to love it."

Elena smiled, leaning her head against his shoulder. "Tomorrow's going to be perfect."

And for that night, it was.

Chapter 7
Four Candles

The sun filtered through the kitchen window in soft golden streams, dancing across the countertops and catching the glitter of wrapping paper scattered like confetti. The scent of vanilla cupcakes warmed the air, and laughter echoed through the modest apartment in New York.

It was the second Saturday in March.

Matthew Colon had just turned four.

He sat at the kitchen table, legs swinging beneath him, his eyes wide with wonder as Elena placed a cupcake in front of him with a single candle that flamed tall and bright. There were already three more cupcakes beside it, each with its candle. Four in total, one for every year he'd filled their lives with light.

Javier stood behind Elena, holding the camcorder. "Okay, champ. Big smile for Daddy."

Matthew grinned, cheeks full, dimples deep, eyes shining like morning. He lifted both arms into the air like a tiny champion. "Cheeeeeeese!"

Click.

Elena chuckled. "You want to make your birthday wish now?"

Matthew nodded and leaned forward, puffing his cheeks.

"Wait," Elena said with a smile. "Close your eyes. You have to believe it for it to come true."

Matthew scrunched his face tight, whispered something only heaven could hear, then blew.

Whooooosh.

Four candles, gone in one breath.

"What'd you wish for?" Javier teased.

Matthew opened one eye. "Can't tell or it won't come true!"

"That's right," Elena said, kissing his curls. "Smart boy."

Javier handed him a wrapped box, about the size of a shoebox but heavier. "This one's from both of us."

Matthew tore into the wrapping, eyes going wide.

Inside was a gleaming red firetruck with working wheels, a siren button, and a tiny extendable ladder. He clutched it with both hands.

"Like the one at the fire station!" he shouted.

"You're our little hero," Elena said.

But then came the biggest surprise.

"Ready for your last present?" Javier said.

He stepped to the front door and wheeled in a big red truck, battery-powered, with chunky black tires, working headlights, and a small horn on the steering wheel. "Jungle Storm" was printed in yellow across the hood.

Matthew gasped. "No way!"

His little hands covered his mouth, and then he sprinted across the living room barefoot, climbing into the truck like a seasoned driver.

"You're the coolest kid in the building now," Javier said proudly.

That afternoon, they took the truck outside into the apartment's parking lot. The sun was bright, the pavement warm. Elena sat on the curb sipping lemonade while Javier adjusted the camcorder again.

Matthew zipped around in the truck, honking and giggling, sunglasses on like he ruled the streets.

"WEE-OOO! WEE-OOO!" he shouted, swerving left and right. "No speeding in my neighborhood!"

A few kids from the complex gathered on the sidewalk, cheering him on.

An older man from the third-floor balcony called down, "Watch out! We got a sheriff in the lot!"

Matthew waved back like he was in a parade.

Elena smiled, her heart full. "He's never coming back inside."

"He's got his wheels now," Javier said. "He's unstoppable."

Matthew honked and pulled into a tight circle, then dramatically "parked" next to the curb.

"Ladies and gentlemen," he shouted, standing in the truck, "I'm four!"

Everyone clapped. He bowed.

That night, after cupcakes, laughter, and reading his favorite book for the third time, Matthew curled up on the couch with his new firetruck in his arms and the red truck parked proudly outside the front door, its tires dusty from a day well lived.

Elena watched her son sleep.

His breathing was steady and slow. His fingers curled around the toy firetruck like it held some invisible magic. His legs, still a little sticky from popsicle juice, kicked gently in his sleep.

Javier came and stood beside her, resting his hand on her shoulder.

"He's amazing," she whispered.

Javier nodded. "God gave us something special."

Elena pressed her fingers to Matthew's cheek, brushing a curl away from his forehead. "I don't ever want this moment to end."

Later, when the apartment was quiet and Matthew was tucked safely into bed, Elena whispered a prayer in the dark:

"Lord, please... protect this child. Let him grow strong and kind. Let him never be far from us. Let him always know he is loved."

Elena closed the door partway and sank onto the sofa, easing into the cushions after a long day. The ceiling fan hummed overhead, carrying the fading scent of vanilla from the kitchen. Voices drifted in through the open window, faint and unfamiliar.

Javier leaned against her, camera in hand, scrolling through the photos he'd taken: the candles, the cheers, the way Matthew's arms shot into the air in pure triumph.

In that moment, there was only joy.

Only love.

Only home.

And in the photograph from that night, it would always be that way.

Chapter 8
Mistaken Identity

Three months later...

"Stay inside the apartment, and don't open the door, Matt. I need to grab the laundry from the basement," Mom said.

Matt didn't lift his eyes from the television. Cartoons flickered on the screen while he clutched his black and green zebra plush.

Ten minutes passed.

She was still gone.

The apartment was quiet.

Matt stood up and walked to the front door. As he slowly opened it, a wave of smoke swept into the room, curling around his face and making him cough.

The hallway was filled with gray haze. Just as he stepped into it, he bumped into Mr. Harvey, who was rushing down the hall.

"Hey, Matt! Where's your mom? We gotta get out of here, kiddo!" Mr. Harvey quickly wrapped his jacket around Matt's head and rushed him toward the stairwell.

Outside, a crowd had gathered. Flames shot from the windows above as the building crackled behind them.

The fire truck arrived moments later, sirens wailing. Firefighters directed people across the street for safety. Mr. Harvey set Matt down near a newspaper stand.

"Wait here, buddy," he said. "I'm going to look for your mom."

Matt clutched his zebra and watched the flashing lights. A familiar voice called his name.

"Hey Matt," said Jose, stepping out from the convenience store. "Where's your mom?"

Matt didn't answer; he rarely did with strangers, but smiled softly. Jose remembered how quiet he usually was.

"C'mon," Jose said gently. He took Matt inside the store and sat him in a chair behind the counter. "You hungry, kiddo?"

Matt nodded, "Yes." Jose gave him a bag of classic potato chips and a bottle of apple juice. He told Matt to stay seated behind the register, so he could go back outside and look for his mom.

Matt continued to eat his potato chips while Jose left the counter.

While standing in the front entrance, Jose was looking and asking the local neighbors if they had seen Elena Colon. Everyone whom he asked said no.

"Hey Darcia, have you seen Elena?" said Jose.

"No, no, I have not seen her," said frantically.

During the fire, Elena exited the building through the back entrance. While outside, an awning from a second-floor window fell on her, leading to a fracture in her right ankle. She was lying in the back alley screaming for help. "Help me, please... help me! Someone, please help me. My son is still inside the building," cried Elena.

After screaming at the top of her lungs, her voice was hoarse. She felt hopeless. "Please let Matt be ok, I'm sorry, Matt," cried Elena. She rested her head on her left arm as she was exhausted from screaming. As Elena closed her eyes to rest for a moment, she heard footsteps approaching. It was Eddie, the homeless guy she always gave a turkey sandwich to in the afternoon when coming home from work. She never knew his name, but he always stood at the corner of the bus stop and her apartment building.

"Miss.....miss, are you ok?" said Eddie.

"Please help me, my leg is stuck," said Elena.

"Ok, I can help you. "I'm going to lift the awning, and you can move your legs.

As Eddie lifted the awning from Elena's leg, she quickly slid her legs free. "Ouch, I think it might be broken," snubbed Elena.

"Can I carry you to the front where the police and fire people are standing?" asked Eddie.

"Please," said Elena. Eddie picked up Elena and carried her through the alley. She wanted to vomit from the smell of not showering for weeks, but she was grateful that he was there at the right moment to help and disregarded the horrific stench. With a soft voice, Elena said, "Thank you so much for helping me."

"Someone help, please help her," shouted Eddie. The EMS team quickly came to Eddie and took Elena, placing her on a gurney. "Ma'am, where are you injured?" said one of the EMS personnel.

"It's my foot; but my son......

"Please help my son, he's four years old, and I think that he is still in the building. I left him in the apartment while I did the laundry. I told him not to open the door," cried Elena. Please check the apartment.

One of the first responders told the Fire Chief that Elena was concerned her child might still be in the apartment. "Which apartment number?

"Apartment, 2B," said Elena.

The Fire Chief radioed for a firefighter to check apartment 2 B. As the firefighter quickly responded to the call, "negative." We already checked the second floor, and no one was found."

One of the firefighters said, "We are making our way through the building. We will double-check, but the building is not going to hold up much longer."

The Fire Chief ordered them to check quickly and exit the building. A few minutes later, all the firefighters had exited, and the fire was extinguished. "I'm sorry, miss, but all residents were able to make it out of the building. We will start asking residents about your son," said the fire chief.

"His name is Matthew Colón, and he's four years old." Her hands searched her pockets out of instinct, as though some proof of him might appear. But she carried nothing, no picture, no papers. Everything was lost to the fire, left behind on the kitchen counter beside the rotary phone as the apartment burned.

Elena was devastated that she could not locate her son or call her husband, who worked the night shift at the packaging company.

"Excuse me, ma'am, but we need to transport you to the hospital to get your leg assessed to make sure it's not broken," said one of the EMS workers.

"No….no, I can't leave my son behind. He is only four years old," cried Elena. She tried to stand, but fell back down immediately.

"Ma'am, please, I think that your foot might be broken."
Screaming and crying frantically, Elena agreed that she needed medical attention, but she couldn't just leave Matt on the streets overnight alone. She started to hyperventilate. The EMS team had to provide oxygen and coached her to calm down.

A few officers came over to the EMS unit to speak with Elena. They got a description of Matthew Colon.

"We are going to canvass the neighborhood and see if anyone has seen him," said one of the female officers.

"Please find him…. please find him," said Elena. Do you have anyone that we could call? "Yes, my husband. He is working, but hopefully, his supervisor will hear the phone ringing. It's loud in the warehouse; they usually have to page him over the intercom."

"What's his work number?" another officer asked.

"555-555-1520."

"We'll call him right away," the sergeant assured her. "We'll have officers begin a search for your son, and we'll meet you at the hospital as soon as possible."

Chapter 9
Good Intentions

Full of fear and desperation, Elena agreed to go to the hospital for an examination. Police officers were clearing the streets and escorting everyone without housing to the nearest shelter for the night.

Meanwhile, Mr. Jose had closed his store early due to the chaos caused by the fire across the street.

"Hey, love, what's for dinner?" Jose asked as he stepped through the front door, exhaustion clinging to his shoulders.

"We're having Salisbury steak, mashed potatoes, and green beans," Georgia called from the kitchen, her voice calm and warm.

But her tone quickly shifted. "Wait a minute, who is this little boy?" she asked, eyes wide as she stepped into the living room.

"This is the lady's child who comes into the store all the time. Their building caught on fire around seven o'clock, and he wandered into the store. I think he got separated from his mother," Jose explained as he gently set the boy down. "His name is Matt."

"Oh, my goodness. She must be worried sick about him," Georgia said, clutching her chest. "Why didn't you take him to the police station?"

"Yeah, I know. I was planning to keep him with us overnight and then take him to the police station first thing in the morning," Jose said. "Let's get him something to eat. I'm pretty sure he's hungry."

"Come here, darling, sit down here," Georgia said, gently guiding Matt to the kitchen table.

She fixed him a small plate of food. After dinner, she gave him a warm bath and dressed him in a pair of her grandson's pajamas. He looked small and vulnerable in an oversized shirt, but he smiled shyly as she tucked him into the toddler-sized Spider-Man bed in the spare bedroom.

The room, still filled with toys and games from their grandchildren's previous visits, had a cozy, comforting atmosphere. Georgia stayed in the room until Matt fell asleep, sitting silently by his side while he clutched his black and green zebra.

She left the door slightly open and made her way to the bedroom. After changing into her nightgown, she lay down next to Jose.

"I hope you can locate his parents tomorrow," Georgia said softly.

"Yeah, me too. Goodnight," Jose replied, his voice weary.

"Goodnight," she echoed, but her mind was filled with worry.

The next morning, Jose woke up around eight o'clock and got dressed to take Matt to the police station. Georgia had already been up for an hour, preparing breakfast for her husband and the little boy.

"What's for breakfast? Everything smells delicious!" Jose said, stepping into the kitchen.

"Good morning, darling! There's toast, eggs, bacon, and pancakes," she replied, her tone cheerful but nervous.

"Let me wake Matt so he can eat before you head out," she said. Georgia walked down the hallway and gently opened the door to the spare bedroom.

Matt was sitting up in bed, playing with a Light-Up Tablet. When he saw her, he smiled.

"Hey, kiddo, do you want to eat breakfast?" Georgia asked kindly.

Matt nodded and set the toy down on the bed. Georgia scooped him up and carried him to the kitchen, sitting him at the table and fixing his plate.

"I hope and pray that you find Matt's parents," Georgia said, glancing at Jose.

"I know, honey," he replied.

"I'm extremely nervous that he's lost. Please, Jose... please find his parents," she said, her voice shaky.

"I'm going to do my best," Jose assured her. "Do you know his mother's name?"

"Yes, I know her first and last name, it's Elena Colon. I don't know her husband's first name. I always addressed him as Mr. Colon," he said, shrugging.

"Oh no! Please describe as much detail as you can when you get to the police station," Georgia urged.

"I will, honey. Don't worry. If anything goes wrong, I'll tell the police I'll keep him with me until they locate his parents," he said, trying to reassure her.

"I have a bad feeling inside my gut," Georgia murmured.

"You worry too much," Jose said, offering her a small smile. "Everything will be fine."

After breakfast, Georgia helped Matt get cleaned up and dressed in fresh clothes. She wanted to wash his dirty ones before returning them to his family.

While putting on Matt's jacket, she noticed something. "Jose... look at this. The name 'Ben' is written on the inside tag."

"I thought you said his name was Matt," she added, confused.

"It is Matt. Why?"

"The tag says Ben. Do they have any other children?"

"No, I've only seen Mrs. Colon with one kid," Jose said. "Don't worry. She probably got the jacket from a second-hand store, or maybe it's a hand-me-down from a cousin. Stop worrying, please."

"Ok, you're right," Georgia sighed, though her eyes lingered on the tag a moment longer.

Jose kissed her on the forehead, grabbed the keys, and headed out the door with Matt. He buckled the boy into his grandson's car seat in the back of his large SUV.

On the way, Jose decided to drive past the remains of the apartment building.

"Oh, my goodness. It's almost to the ground," he whispered.

Matt didn't seem to notice; he was busy twisting his black and green zebra in the air and making playful noises.

"We're here, kiddo! Let's go find your mommy," Jose said as he parked outside the police station.

He carried Matt inside and approached the front desk. "Hi there, officer. I'm here to find this kid's parents."

The officer looked up from his computer and took Jose's contact information. As he was writing, he asked, "So, this boy is not your son or any relation to you?"

"No, I know him from the neighborhood. He and his mother come into my store regularly. He was wandering around last night during the fire."

"Are you referring to the fire on the corner of West Market Street and 15th?" the officer asked.

"Yes, I own Mini Mart, across the street from the apartment building."

"I'm familiar with your store," the officer nodded, then gestured for Jose to follow him. "Let's head to Detective Reagan's desk to take your statement."

"Where are you taking Matt?" Jose asked.

"He'll stay with the social worker and another officer while we work on finding his parents. It's protocol."

Jose nodded reluctantly and followed the officer to the detective's desk. He sat across from Detective Reagan, who welcomed him.

"How are you doing today, sir?"

"I'm well. I'm just trying to ensure this little boy finds his way back to his family. He got separated during the fire last night."

"That building is likely going to be condemned. It sustained significant damage to the foundation, partially collapsed roof," Reagan commented.

"Yeah, I saw it on the way here," Jose agreed. "Not much left."

"Alright, I need to ask you some questions. How did you come across the boy?"

Jose explained everything, how he had seen the fire, noticed Matt walking alone, recognized him from the store, and taken him in for the night.

"Why didn't you bring him here last night?"

"The police asked everyone to close early. I left through the back alley. I was planning to bring him this morning. He was already shaken."

"Understood. I'll speak with officers from last night to see if any reports came in."

As Detective Reagan stepped away, Jose glanced at the front desk and noticed another couple reporting a missing child. "What's going on in the city today?" he murmured.

He caught a glimpse of Matt in the interview room, seated with a social worker and an officer.

At the front desk, Emma and Andres Diaz looked like a couple who had been through a sleepless night. Emma's hair was tucked beneath a brown wig, a knitted beanie pulled low over her forehead. Andres wore a baseball cap, the brim shadowing his eyes. Both smelled faintly of smoke.

Andres clutched a creased photo of a small boy, Ben, gripped so tightly that the edges bent beneath his fingers. His voice wavered as he spoke to the officer on duty.

"We're staying at the Harbor View Inn," he said, gesturing vaguely toward the street beyond. "It's right next to the apartment building that caught fire last night. We… we were in the courtyard when the alarms went off."

Emma sniffled, her hands twisting in the sleeves of her sweater. "Ben was on the swings by the little playground. We thought we had him, but when people started running and shouting…" She broke off, her voice catching.

Andres picked up the thread. "There was smoke everywhere. Police officers were shouting to clear the streets. We couldn't see him through the crowd. We searched around the inn, the parking lot, the street…nothing. He's shy, Officer. He wouldn't just run off."

Emma's eyes brimmed with tears. "We…we're from Indiana. We just came to see the Statue of Liberty, that's all."

This was supposed to be a happy trip, and now…" She pressed her hand to her mouth.

The officer nodded sympathetically, jotting down notes. "Last place you saw him?"

Emma's voice trembled. "Near the swings. Black-and-green zebra jacket, gray sweatpants, blue sneakers. He's only four. Please… please find him."

The officer assured them that patrols were searching the area. Emma and Andres sat on the worn bench by the door, holding hands tightly.

Later, Detective Reagan returned to Jose. "Good news. We've located Matt's parents. His mom broke her leg during the fire, and Mr. Colon is on his way. Thank you for taking care of him."

"That's a relief," Jose said, exhaling. "Can I go now?"

"Yes, thank you again."

As Jose left, Emma stood from her seat in the corner. She leaned toward Andres. "Honey, I need to use the restroom."

She walked down the hall past the waiting area and froze.

There he was. Sitting in a chair next to a uniformed officer, small hands folded in his lap, eyes darting nervously around the room.

"Ben?" she breathed, her voice trembling just enough to sound genuine. She rushed forward. "Honey, when did you get here?"

The social worker quickly stood. "Ma'am, please step back. This child is in our care."

Emma clutched her chest. "In your care? This is my son…Benjamin Diaz!"

The officer frowned. "Ma'am, his name is Matthew Colon. We're waiting for his father to arrive."

Emma's hand shot into her bag. "No…look!" She pulled out a worn photograph. In it, a boy in a black and green zebra jacket grinned at the camera. She pointed quickly. "That's this jacket…see? And the tag inside still has its name. Ben. Check it yourself!"

The social worker hesitated, glancing at the officer. The tag was checked. The name was there.

Andres appeared at Emma's side, voice firm but calm. "That's our boy. We've been here all morning filing the report. He must've gotten turned around in all the confusion after the fire."

Emma's eyes brimmed with tears. "We thought we'd lost him forever."

After a brief huddle between the officer and social worker—too quickly, too trusting, they nodded.

"All right. We'll release him into your care."

Emma dropped to her knees, hugging Matthew tightly. "Mommy's here. Mommy's got you."

Emma gripped Matthew's hand tightly as she and Andres stepped through the station's front doors. A gust of cold air met them, carrying the blare of sirens from somewhere down the street. People streamed in and out of the entrance: officers, bystanders, parents holding children close.

Across the lot, a dark sedan swerved into a parking space. Its driver, eyes locked on the building, slammed the door shut behind him and started toward the entrance.

Emma kept her head down, tugging Matthew toward the far side of the lot. She didn't look back.

And Javier Colon, moving quickly through the crowd, didn't look to his left.

Chapter 10
A Tragic Error

Javier's pulse raced as he pushed through the police station doors, scanning every corner of the lobby for his son. He had come to bring Matt home; his heart clung to the hope that this nightmare would finally end here.

But when he reached the front desk, the officer's expression told him something was wrong.

"What do you mean you don't have him?" Javier asked, confusion cracking in his voice. "I was told someone brought him in this morning."

Detective Reagan stepped in, his tone steady but guarded. "Another couple came in this morning. They reported their son missing, the same age, the same build. They brought a photo, and he looked very similar to the child we had here. He was wearing a black and green zebra jacket, with a name written inside the tag."

Javier's stomach knotted. "What name?"

"Ben."

The word made his chest tighten.

Javier lifted the receiver of the desk phone, the cord tangling around his wrist as he dialed the hospital's main number. After a moment, a crisp operator's voice answered.

"City Hospital, how may I direct your call?"

"I need to speak with Elena Colon," Javier said, his throat dry.

"One moment."

The line clicked, then went silent for a long pause, followed by the faint buzz of the transfer. At last, another voice came through, soft and trembling.

"Hello?"

"Elena?"

She sounded exhausted, her words fragile as paper. "Yes… It's me."

"Elena, what was Matt wearing last night?"

"His Spider-Man T-shirt, red jogger pants, and…" Her voice slowed. "…a black and green zebra jacket. The one I got from the second-hand store last week."

Her breath caught. "Javier… what's going on? Where's Matt?"

"I'm still trying to figure that out. Stay calm for me, okay?" His voice was breaking, but he forced the words out.

"I'll call you back."

Javier clutched the phone, listening to the dead line a moment longer before hanging up.

He returned slowly, each step deliberate. His hands covered his face.

"They let my baby go with strangers," he whispered. "How could this happen?" Javier sat on the bench, distressed.

Detective Reagan stepped into the hallway as the desk phone rang. He lifted the receiver, the coiled cord stretching as he pressed it to his ear.

On the other end, an officer's voice came through, flat and urgent.

"Sir, we've got a juvenile victim at Cedar Blue Park. Creek bed. Approximate age: four to five years old. Male. Wearing gray sweatpants and a black and green zebra jacket."

Reagan's grip on the receiver tightened. "Condition?"

A pause. "Unresponsive. Fatal head trauma. It appears as if he fell from the cliff near the playground. Coroner's already on scene. They'll be transporting the body shortly."

Reagan exhaled, then glanced back toward the office where Javier sat slumped at the desk, his hands gripping his knees, eyes frantic.

"I will meet with the coroner shortly," Reagan instructed. "I'm on my way."

He returned to Javier, his voice heavy. "Excuse me, I need to go immediately." An officer will stay with you."

Javier's brow furrowed.

Reagan gave a tight nod. "Don't worry, we are not disregarding your case."

Javier's leg bounced nervously. "Please. Just find my son."

Reagan and Chaser moved quickly toward the exit. Outside, the siren came alive, fading into the distance as Javier sat hunched in the hard plastic chair, head in his hands.

Thirty minutes later, Detective Reagan and Lt. Chaser pulled into the coroner's lot. The air inside was cold, heavy with antiseptic, the hum of the fluorescent lights filling the silence.

On a stainless-steel table, a small body lay beneath a white sheet.

"We need to confirm the identity," the coroner said gently.

Reagan gave a single nod. The coroner folded the sheet back, revealing a pale, still face. Reagan's jaw tensed.

"Where did you find him?" he asked quietly. "And… what happened to his face?"

"In the creek at Cedar Blue Park on the south end," the coroner replied. "Looks like a fall from the cliff. The head trauma was fatal. He'd been submerged most of the night."

Reagan absorbed the words without speaking.

Turning to Chaser, the coroner added, "We'll need you to run his description against all active missing child reports."

Chaser pulled out his notepad, already jotting down the clothing, age range, and location. "We'll start the cross-reference now."

The coroner replaced the sheet, and Reagan exchanged a quiet word with Chaser before stepping out into the crisp air of the parking lot. The child's identity was still unknown.

Back at the police station, Javier sat alone on the hard, plastic bench, the fluorescent lights overhead buzzing faintly. Their cold glare cast a sterile wash over everything, but nothing could sterilize the chaos inside his soul.

His trembling hands clutched Matthew's tiny blue jacket, the one he'd found crumpled in the back seat of the car. The fabric still smelled like him: sunlight, apples, and the faintest trace of baby shampoo. He buried his face in it and wept silently, unwilling to let the world see the storm ripping through him.

Every second stretched into a cruel eternity. Time didn't just slow; it taunted him. The wall clock ticked too loudly, too steadily, indifferent to his breaking heart.

He kept replaying it, how quickly it all happened. The phone call. The smoke. The chaos. And then nothing. One moment, his son was lying in bed asleep, and the next... gone.

Now he sat here, pleading with officers who offered little more than practiced sympathy and procedural updates. No confirmation. No comfort. No answers.

Javier didn't know how long he'd been sitting there, the jacket gripped tight in his hands, when the door to the station opened, and Detective Reagan walked in.

Javier bolted to his feet, hope rising like a gasp in his chest. But the detective didn't meet his eyes.

"We believe your son may have already been claimed... by another family."

The words slammed into him. "What do you mean by ' claimed?" Javier's voice cracked. "He's not a coat in a lost and found. That's my son."

Lt. Chaser shifted, uncomfortable but firm. "A couple came in earlier. They said they had lost their son in the chaos, too. Paperwork's being processed."

Javier staggered back a step, his legs barely holding him. "That's not possible. You let him go? You gave him away without checking?"

It was too late. Somewhere, strangers were holding his boy. Somewhere, a mistake, or a lie, had stolen what was most precious to him.

He collapsed back onto the bench, numb with horror. His arms ached to hold Matthew, but they were empty. His heart screamed, but no one heard.

Later, outside the precinct, panic swallowed him whole. He had called out Matthew's name until his throat burned raw, the sound echoing down the street. Bystanders stopped in their tracks, watching as a father pleaded with the sky.

He didn't know how to tell Elena.

In the front seat of his car, faith cracked, and hope slipped away. Inside his chest, a silent war raged between believing he would find his son again... and fearing that he already hadn't. He turned the key, the engine rumbling to life, and drove toward the hospital.

Chapter 11
The Empty Space Where He Should Be

While Elena waited for Javier to return to the hospital, she felt something was wrong. Not just wrong... unnatural. A mother knows. Her body knew. Her chest ached in a way no inhalation of smoke could explain. Her arms, empty, hung at her sides like they'd failed the only task they were made for: holding him.

Javier arrived, eyes bloodshot.

"Where's Matt? Javier, where's our son?"

Javier couldn't speak. Elena's scream echoed down the hospital corridor.

"No! That's not possible! He was watching television when I left. How could he end up in someone's arms?" she cried. "Something is wrong. Please take me to the precinct. I need answers for myself."

Javier tried to comfort her, but she pushed him away.

"Leave me alone. I should have stayed with him. I am sorry, Javier. I'm so sorry."

She wept.

"It's not your fault," he whispered.

Elena rocked in the hospital bed, repeating through tears, "It's my fault. I could not move. The awning trapped me. I couldn't find him."

Elena gasped. She tried to stand, but her legs gave out.

Once discharged from the hospital, Javier helped Elena into the car. He drove back to the police station. Now, she stood on crutches in the local precinct's lobby, her hands clenched at her sides, staring through the glass doors like she could wish her son to appear. Elena's skin smelled like ash, her blouse was stained from the alley's gravel and wrinkled, but none of that mattered. All she cared about was Matthew. Elena stood at the front desk screaming, "Where's my son?"

"Ma'am, please," the young officer behind the desk said again, his voice steady but not kind. "We're doing everything we can. We've already alerted other precincts, nearby hospitals, emergency shelters..."

"That's not enough!" she snapped, her voice cracking under its weight. "That is not enough! He is four years old! His name is Matthew Javier Colon. He has a tiny scar above his right eyebrow."

Tears clung to her lashes but refused to fall. She wouldn't give them that. Not yet.

"Mrs. Colon," came another voice, softer, older: a woman, a mother herself. "I know this is the worst moment of your life, but we're going to need you to answer a few more questions. We under..."

"Don't you dare say you understand," Elena interrupted, the words spilling like acid. "Because if you understood, you wouldn't be calm. If your child vanished in front of your eyes, you wouldn't be standing here like this!"

She slammed her palm against the counter, startling the officer. The woman flinched. Elena didn't care. Rage had replaced reason. Her son was out there alone, scared, and all these uniforms could do was fill out forms.

She could hear his voice shaking behind the glass doors of the waiting area, begging someone, anyone, to give him good news.

Elena's heart was a war zone, grief battling guilt, hope clashing with horror. Every time the precinct doors opened, she turned with wild, breathless urgency. And every time it was not Matthew, her stomach sank lower.

She thought about the last thing she had said to him the previous morning, before the fire.

"Let Mama zip your coat, baby, it's cold."

Had she kissed him?

God, had she kissed him?

She could not remember.

Then a young officer stepped out from the back room, clipboard in hand, face unreadable. Elena moved before he even called her name.

"Yes? Did you find him? Is he here?"

The officer blinked, almost surprised by her swiftness. "Ma'am... I need you to take a seat."

Her blood ran cold.

Javier returned to her side, chest heaving, his voice raw. "What is it? What's going on?"

The officer shifted uncomfortably. "Earlier this morning, a family came in.... She said he was their son. He matched the general description and..."

"What do you mean?" Elena cried. "You gave our son to strangers?"

The air left her lungs like a punch to the chest. She swayed, and Javier caught her, wrapping an arm around her waist to steady her in the chair. But she could not feel it. Her body was numb. Her mind, burning.

"They took him?"

The officer held up his hands. "There was confusion. Chaos. The child responded to the name they gave Ben. He was dazed but unharmed. The couple had documentation… they were distraught, convincing…"

"You were supposed to protect him!" she screamed. "You were supposed to verify, not just assume. That's our baby!"

The room quieted around her. Other parents. Other survivors. The whispers began. None of it mattered.

She slid to the floor and curled into herself, rocking slightly, her arms crossed over her stomach as she could somehow hold the empty place where Matthew should be. "No, no, no… God, please…"

Javier crouched beside her, tears streaming silently down his face, his voice barely audible: "We'll get him back. We'll find him. I promise you."

But Elena didn't believe him. Not while her baby boy was out there calling another woman 'Mommy.'

In that moment, she realized something terrible.

The fire didn't take her son.

The silence did.

The silence that followed after, when no one corrected the mistake. When no one looked harder. When grief became bureaucracy.

And as the precinct doors closed again behind another shift change. They left the police station without Matt. The ride was silent until they reached the doorstep of his parents' home.

Inside, Javier's mother wept, clutching Elena tightly as if she could hold her together. His father stood frozen in the doorway, helpless. Elena eventually tore free, fleeing down the narrow hallway. A door slammed, her screams echoing through the house.

The faded floral couch sagged beneath his mother as she sank into it, the hum of the old box fan in the window filling the silence between sobs. On the kitchen wall, the beige rotary phone hung unused, its coiled cord swaying slightly, as if mocking its uselessness now.

Javier dropped into a chair. "I don't know how we're going to survive this."

His mother took his face in her hands. "We will. We must. We cannot let grief steal our faith."

Javier's voice broke. "We've lost our home… and our son." He buried his face in his hands and wept heavily.

His parents embraced him. "You can stay with us until you find a place," his father said.

For a moment, no one spoke. The only sound was Elena's muffled sobs from down the hall. Javier felt the crushing weight of loss pressing on his chest, yet in his parents' arms, there was a flicker of warmth, a reminder that not everything had been taken. Somewhere beneath the grief, a fragile thread of hope still held.

They would cling to it, together, until the day God saw fit to lead them back to their boy.

Chapter 12
A Name Without a Face

By sunrise, Detective Reagan had already made three calls to Child Protective Services, flagged every intake report from the tri-state area, and sent out a region-wide bulletin for any unidentified children matching Matthew Colon's description. The precinct was humming, the tension unmistakable. Every officer knew they were sitting in the shadow of a grave mistake, and no one wanted their name on the final report.

"Do we have anything on the creek incident yet?" Chaser asked as he entered the coroner's basement level, where the exam room was located. He rubbed his bloodshot eyes and took a deep breath to brace for the worst.

The coroner looked up from his clipboard, shaking his head. "Male, approximately five years old. The cause of death appears to be blunt force trauma. No visible signs of prior abuse. No identification, and there's no missing person report matching his description."

Chaser's jaw tightened. "Fingerprints?"

"Ran them through, nothing. Too young to have anything on file. We'll try dental records, but at his age, that's a long shot."

"What about DNA?"

The coroner exhaled. "We can send a sample to the state lab, but it won't be quick. It could take weeks before anything comes back. Chaser cursed under his breath. "So, we've got a deceased boy with no name and a missing boy who was wrongly released. And we need to canvas the neighborhood."

In the days following Matthew's disappearance, the department shifted into overdrive. A command post was set up in the precinct's conference room, with maps of the city pinned and marked in red to show possible sightings. Officers worked in rotating shifts, canvassing nearby neighborhoods, knocking on doors, and stopping pedestrians.

Pairs of officers carried grainy stills printed from the precinct's surveillance footage, one frame showing a man and a woman walking out with Matthew between them, his small hand tightly clutched in the woman's grasp.

On the east side, Officers Ramirez and Doyle approached an older man sweeping the sidewalk outside a corner bodega. Doyle held out the photo.

"Sir, have you seen these people before?"

The man squinted, adjusting his cap. "That looks like... maybe Andrés Diaz. I knew him from Elmore Apartments. Not sure about the woman, photo's too fuzzy to see her face. But... I'll tell you this, about two nights ago, they loaded up a large SUV in the dark. Left before sunrise. No goodbye, no notice to the landlord."

Ramirez jotted notes while Doyle asked, "They have a kid with them?"

The man hesitated, then nodded toward the apartments across the street. "Ask Mr. Hollis in 3 B. He's been complaining about the noise up there for months."

Mr. Hollis, a retired dockworker with a weathered face, answered after the third knock. His voice was low and uneasy. "I don't like to get involved in other folks' business, but I saw something... The boy. He was crying by the window, banging on the glass like he was scared out of his mind, and it happened earlier this week. Next thing, the woman came, yanked him back, and shut the curtains. Didn't see him after that."

When pressed, Hollis admitted he never called the police. "Thought it was just a family argument."

Later that afternoon in the department briefing room, Lieutenant Chaser stood at the head of the packed room, the fluorescent lights humming above. The mood was heavy, tension hanging like a storm cloud. A large corkboard displayed side-by-side photos: one of Matthew Colon, the other of the unidentified boy pulled from the creek. Between them, crime scene stills of the couple walking Matthew out of the precinct.

"Alright, listen up," Chaser began, his voice firm. "Let's call this what it is, an abduction under the guise of a reunification. We may have experienced a custodial oversight or a breakdown in our verification protocols. If this couple forged documents, we're looking at identity fraud, endangering the welfare of a child, and possibly kidnapping."

Detective Ramos stepped forward with his notes. "We spoke with two separate witnesses at Elmore Apartments. Both confirm seeing a boy in the couple's unit within the last week. One saw the child crying and banging on the window. The couple allegedly moved out in the middle of the night, taking a large SUV. No forwarding address."

Officer Doyle added, "Neighbors say the man is likely Andrés Diaz. They're less certain about the woman, but we have a partial match to an Emma Diaz in DMV records. We're pulling her old license photo for visual confirmation."

Chaser nodded. "Good. Keep pushing…canvass businesses along possible exit routes: gas stations, motels, toll booths. Someone saw them, and someone has them on tape. Find it."

He turned back to the board, tapping the photos. "We have got two families. Two stories. And one gaping hole in the truth. Until we confirm the identity of the child seen in that apartment, we don't know the boy from the creek's identity, but we are looking into it. And I do not care how far they've gone, we're going to find them."

The room erupted in the rustle of chairs and clipped "Yes, sir" replies as officers gathered their folders and rushed back out into the field. The hunt was officially on.

Despite the department's full-court press, every promising lead dissolved into smoke. Witness tips a dead-end. The large SUV sighting went nowhere. And there were no surveillance cameras in the wooded stretch where the boy's body was found.

The only closure came on one point: the fire that had displaced the Colon family, along with dozens of other residents, was ruled accidental, the result of faulty wiring.

In the days that followed, Lt. Chaser kept working long after the building went dark. Three nights in a row, it was just him, a desk lamp, and the stale bite of cold coffee. He reread statements. Rewatched footage. Reconstructed timelines until the edges blurred.

And still, nothing.

The trail had gone cold.

His gaze drifted back to the two photographs pinned above his desk: the Colon family picture, Matthew's grin wide, brown eyes, and full of life, and the stark crime scene photo of the boy pulled from the creek, wearing a shirt with "Ben Diaz" stitched inside the collar.

His chest tightened.

This wasn't over. Not by a long shot.

Chaser pulled a blank notepad from his drawer and, in thick black ink, scrawled three words across the top:

Find the truth.

Without hesitation, he picked up the phone and dialed a private number, a forensics contact who owed him a favor.

Because somewhere out there, someone knew what happened to Matthew Colon and the boy from the creek.

And Lt. Chaser and Detective Reagan had no intention of stopping until they uncovered it.

Chapter 13
A Whisper in the Noise

Detective Reagan was halfway out of his chair, the weight of failure clinging to his shoulders like a wet coat, when the precinct doors creaked open.

"Yo," a gruff voice called from the front. "I need to talk to someone about the kid. The one who went missing."

Lt. Chaser turned. The man at the threshold looked like he hadn't slept in days, with leathered skin, deep-set eyes, and a faded hoodie pulled tight against the summer heat. Recognition came instantly.

Jose Ramos. Business owner. A man with deep roots and deeper connections, always with a line to the underground.

"Matthew Colon," Jose said, stepping inside. "I heard he didn't just go missing. I heard he was taken."

That single word taken, froze Chaser mid-step.

He waved Jose toward his desk. "Start talking."

Jose glanced around as if the walls themselves could betray him. "Word on the block is... somebody messed up in here. Real bad. Said the kid got handed over to some couple who weren't even his people."

Chaser's jaw locked. "Who told you that?"

"People talk, man," Jose said, shrugging. "After the fire, everybody thought it was just a tragedy. But then someone said that this lady, Emma Diaz, and her husband showed up here claiming a boy who wasn't theirs. Next thing you know, her place is empty. Vanished overnight."

Chaser exhaled through his nose, fighting the burn of anger. "Where did they live?"

"Elmore Apartments. And I'm telling you, Lieutenant, you all got played. Street's saying this place gave a missing kid to a woman who's not right in the head. Some folks think she's done this before."

That last part made Chaser's stomach drop. "Before?"

Jose nodded. "About a year ago. Rumors about a boy gone missing in Jersey. The same woman's name came up. People thought it was just street gossip, but now..." He trailed off, shaking his head. "Now it looks different."

"This isn't just a mistake," Chaser muttered. "This is a pattern."

"Can you give me names?" he asked.

Jose hesitated, chewing on his bottom lip. "Not on paper. But I'll point you to the right person to talk to. Just don't say it came from me."

"You came in here," Chaser said quietly. "That counts for something."

Jose stared down at the linoleum. "That boy, Matthew, he's just a kid. He didn't deserve this."

Chaser nodded once, firmly. "No. He didn't."

He turned toward the whiteboard, eyes scanning the old case notes and photographs. With a marker, he began crossing out dead ends and drawing new lines: New Jersey, missing boy,

Andrés and Emma Diaz. The board came alive with fresh direction.

The department might've failed once. He wouldn't let it happen again.

This wasn't just a missing persons case anymore.

This was criminal.

He picked up his desk phone and began dialing the first lead Jose had given him. Somewhere out there, Matthew was still alive, and Chaser intended to bring him home.

Chapter 14
Buried Things Do Not Stay Buried

Two weeks later.

"We need to find that couple."

Chaser's voice cut through the morning static in the precinct's briefing room. The whiteboard was now a battlefield, with old driving license photos of Andrés and Emma Diaz, Matthew Colon, and the unidentified boy from the creek. Arrows, timelines, red string, it looked less like a missing persons board now and more like the unraveling blueprint of a fractured family.

Detective Reagan stood beside Chaser, both men wearing the exhaustion of too many nights without sleep. The Diaz case had grown from an internal embarrassment into a statewide search.

Every hour Matthew remained missing, the margin for saving him shrank.

The News broadcast went out across New York on billboards and scrolling news crawlers.

The Colon family watched it all unfold in real time. Elena sat beside Javier on the couch, eyes locked on the screen but seeing something far older, her son's gap-toothed smile in the rearview mirror, his voice singing from the back seat.

That evening, Elena stopped by the mini mart without a shopping list. She just needed air.

Jose was behind the counter, unpacking soup cans.

"You okay?" he asked without looking up.

"I don't know anymore," she admitted.

He looked up, eyes softening. "I've been praying for him. For all of you."

Her voice caught. "Thank you… for speaking up. You didn't have to."

"Couldn't live with myself if I didn't," Jose said.

She left empty-handed but heavy-hearted.

The next morning, Chaser and Reagan stood outside an aging house in New Jersey with three other officers. The address had come from a back-channel tip, one of Jose's old contacts who remembered the Diaz family before they vanished.

The neighborhood was still, overgrown, and silent in the way only abandoned places can be. A rusting tricycle lay on its side in the yard. The blinds were shut tight.

"Looks empty," Chaser said. He tried the door, but it was locked.

The battering ram changed that.

Inside, the air was stale, heavy with the smell of damp fabric. Half-folded laundry sat on the couch. Dishes floated in cloudy sink water. Family photos had been ripped from the walls, leaving pale rectangles on faded paint.

"Looks like they left in a hurry," one officer muttered.

They swept the house room by room until a voice echoed from below.

"Lieutenant! You need to see this."

Chaser followed the sound into the unfinished basement, lit only by a single bare bulb, and in the corner sat a rusted top-loading washing machine, its lid half open.

He lifted it entirely and froze. Inside, curled like a discarded doll, were the remains of a small child.

Within the hour, the county coroner and state investigators were on scene. The coroner crouched beside the machine, his voice low.

"Male, about four or five years old. Early signs suggest he'd been in water for a long time before being placed here. I'll confirm after the autopsy."

Chaser's voice was rough. "Why a washing machine?"

The coroner shook his head. "I've seen people do strange things when they panic. That's all I can say for now."

Back at the precinct, Chaser spread the thin case file across his desk. The coroner's notes were blunt: Unidentified Male. Approx. Age: 4–5. Cause of death pending.

No ID. No fingerprints. Nothing that could give the child a name.

The hospital fax came first. One verified record: Jacob Diaz. Male infant. SIDS. Deceased, 1988.

But Jacob wasn't the boy in the washing machine.

Chaser dug deeper. Birth and pediatric records listed two more children under Emma and Andrés Diaz: Carlos, born in 1990, and Ben, born in 1991. Both had routine checkups on file, but no death certificates. No closures.

Three children on paper. Only one confirmed dead.

Chaser leaned back, rubbing his temples. He wrote the name "Jacob" across the board in thick marker. Carlos. Ben. Then, he drew a hard circle around the last two.

"Instead of calling for help, Emma and Andrés panicked," he muttered grimly. "And now a boy is dead. But which one?"

Chapter 15
Running from the Past

Meanwhile, as Lt. Chaser and Detective Reagan pushed deeper into the case, across town, Andrés and Emma Diaz were holed up in a dimly lit roadside motel. The carpet smelled of mildew, and the air was heavy with stale cigarette smoke and unwashed clothes. For nearly three weeks, they had been living like shadows, keeping the curtains drawn, stepping outside only when necessary, and never using the same route twice.

The missing child bulletins had rattled them. Matthew's photo was plastered on telephone poles, taped to the windows of corner stores, and printed in the back pages of the daily paper. The evening news ran his picture between weather and sports, the anchor's voice urging anyone with information to call the police. Patrol cars lingered longer on certain streets now, and Emma swore she saw the same unmarked sedan twice in one day.

Andrés sat on the edge of the bed, chain-smoking and staring at the muted television. Emma paced the small room, arms wrapped tightly around herself. Every knock from the neighboring room made her flinch. Every set of footsteps in the hallway felt like they were coming for them.

"They're closing in," she whispered, her voice thin. "I can feel it." Andrés crushed his cigarette into an overflowing ashtray and lit another. "We keep our heads down, no phone calls. No visitors. We wait until it blows over."

Emma had been pacing for hours, tugging at her sleeves, muttering to herself. Andrés sat on the edge of the bed, eyes fixed on the muted television, lost in thought.

"We need to turn ourselves in, Emma," Andrés said at last, his voice tight with fear. "We can say it was a mistake, mistaken identity. It'll go smoother if we come clean now. I don't want to go to jail."

"We won't go to jail if we stick to the plan," Emma snapped, her eyes darting like trapped birds. "I've already lost three children. I'm not going to lose this one, too."

Andrés's shoulders sagged, the fight draining out of him. He bent over, retching again, the bitter taste of bile burning his throat. When he finally straightened, his face was pale, his hands shaking.

"Emma…" His voice trembled, breaking against the words. "You're not well. This isn't normal."

"I think you're carrying something deep like PTSD, maybe worse. From Jacob. From Carlos. From Ben. It's eating you alive… and if you don't get help, I'm afraid of what will happen."

"No!" she screamed. "You don't get to say that! You weren't there when Carlos fell off the banister. His little body twisted like a rag doll. I screamed and screamed, but he wouldn't wake up. I… I panicked." Her voice cracked, dropping to a whisper. "And when Ben… when Ben drowned in the bathtub, it was because I left him. I heard the crash downstairs, Carlos fell, and I just… forgot Ben was in the water."

Emma collapsed onto the bed, clutching a pillow to her chest. "By the time I got back, he was already floating face down in the water. I couldn't save him."

Andrés rubbed his face, anguish carved deep in the lines around his eyes. "Why didn't you call the police?"

"I didn't know what to do," Emma whispered, trembling. "I wrapped him in a towel. I rocked him. But… he was gone. I put him in the washing machine before we left that night because… because I couldn't look at him like that anymore." Her face crumpled, tears streaking her cheeks. "I didn't kill him, Andrés. It was an accident."

"But then I saw that boy at the mall, he looked just like Ben. I thought maybe… maybe God was giving me another chance."

Andrés turned away, his fists curling tight. "That boy was not Ben. He had a family. And this child has a family, too. We can't just pretend…"

"He is Ben!" she shouted, voice cracking. "He has Ben's eyes. His laugh. His little voice, he called me Mommy."

"He didn't, Emma." Andrés's tone was flat, exhausted. "You told him to.

Silence pressed between them. Emma stared at the wall, her breathing shallow. Then, in a whisper, "We can start over. We'll move to Florida. We can change our identities. I can dye my hair, and we can stay under the radar. He'll forget. He's just a child."

Andrés felt the familiar pull of guilt, love, and fear. Slowly, he nodded. "Pack your things."

They left the motel in the dead of night, headlights off until they reached the highway. Every car in the rearview felt like a patrol unit. Every passing billboard looked like it could flash their faces at any second.

They drove south for hours, stopping only for gas, until they reached Florida. They found a modest townhouse in a quiet suburban neighborhood. Andrés took a job at a small real estate agency; Emma found part-time work as a secretary at a small trucking company, which paid under the table. On the surface, they appeared to be a normal family. Behind closed doors, the lie grew heavier.

Emma dressed Matthew in Ben's old clothes. She cut his hair the same way. Every morning, she made his lunch and walked him to daycare, introducing him as "Ben."

One morning at breakfast, she called him to the table.

"Ben, honey, come eat."

Matthew didn't move. Still in his pajamas, he clutched a toy truck in the living room.

"My name is Matt," he said firmly.

Emma's hands trembled. "Oh, sweetheart, your name is Ben. But it's okay, we can call you Matt for a little while."

"No," he cried. "I want to go home."

Emma's face twisted. "Can't I be your mommy for a little bit? Just until you remember how much I love you?"

Matthew ran to the corner, sobbing. Andrés walked in, frowning.

"What's going on?"

"Nothing," Emma said too quickly. "He's just adjusting."

Later that day, Emma dropped Matt off at daycare. She told Ms. Carter, "He likes to be called Matt now. It's from a book we read. He connected with the character."

Ms. Carter smiled. "That's sweet."

Emma left, but her hands shook as she gripped the steering wheel. What if Matt said something? What if someone looked too closely?

At work, she was in a daze, her mind replaying Matthew's words from this morning. Then her boss, Derek, snapped from across the room.

"Emma, the phone's ringing. Again."

She was startled. "Sorry. I'm... distracted."

Derek sighed. "You need to learn to leave your personal life at home."

She nodded, eyes glazed, but inside she burned. He's watching me. He knows. They all know. They want to take my son.

In her head, she heard Ben's voice: Mommy, I'm cold.

The hum of the office printer filled the silence steadily, rhythmically, like the washing machine. Her fingers twitched.

That night, Emma sat on the couch, rocking back and forth, holding one of Ben's old shirts to her face. Andrés entered quietly.

"I saw the news," he said, his voice low but urgent. "They showed your face, Emma, an old driver's license photo from five years ago."

Emma's gaze drifted past him, fixed on nothing. Her expression was glassy, unbothered. "I don't care. I was younger then... I looked different. That's perfect."

Andrés stepped closer, his pulse quickening. "We need to go further. Maybe Miami. Or out west."

She finally looked at him, the corner of her mouth twitching into something between a smile and a sneer. "No. We're staying in Jacksonville. They won't find us."

"He'll remember, Emma. He's started repeating his name."

"We protect our family," she said flatly. "No one will take him from me; he's my child."

Andrés sat beside her. For a moment, they said nothing.

"I miss the real Ben," he whispered.

Emma turned to him. "I see him every day."

The next morning, she packed sandwiches, her hands trembling as she sang softly under her breath. "You are my light, my only light..."

Matthew stood by the door, holding a drawing. It showed a woman, a man, and a little boy holding hands. The woman had brown hair. Emma was blonde.

"Who is this?" she asked, her voice sharp.

"My real mommy," said Matt.

Emma's vision blurred. Her knees buckled. "No," she muttered. "I'm your mommy."

Matt stepped back. Andrés entered, saw the drawing, and the look on Emma's face. He knew they were close to the edge.

"Maybe... we need to stop," he said carefully.

Emma stood, her eyes dark. "You were never meant to be a father. You gave up on Jacob. On Carlos. On Ben. And now you want to give up on him?"

"I want to give him back."

Emma turned away. In the mirror, she swore she saw Jacob, Carlos, and Ben. They smiled. It's okay, Mommy, the vision whispered. You'll get it right this time.

She smiled back.

Andrés watched in silence, knowing he was living with a woman slowly unraveling. Their past was catching up. The names they buried, the lies they told, everything was clawing its way back to the surface. And deep down, he knew the illusion wouldn't hold forever.

Chapter 16
Florida

Emma had learned to smile through the cracks. But beneath the calm surface, the same storms were brewing, just waiting for a place to break.

It had been two years since Emma and Andrés fled north under the cover of night, settling quietly in Jacksonville after a new broadcast splashed their faces across half the state. They'd built a life that looked ordinary from the outside. But behind closed doors, the lies were still alive, and so was Emma's obsession.

Matt was now six years old. That morning, after dropping him at school, Emma sat at her desk, daydreaming about her real children, Jacob, Carlos, and Ben, and wishing she could see them again.

"Emma, take your break. When you come back in an hour, maybe you'll be more focused on work," Derek snapped, irritation sharp in his voice.

She forced a polite smile and headed to the small break room, sliding into a seat across from Jackie and Kelly.

"Hey, Emma, what's going on?" Jackie asked, peeling back the lid on her yogurt.

Emma nodded toward Kelly. "Hi, Ladies. I'm just tired of Derek's annoying attitude."

"He's always like that before lunch," Kelly said. "Hey, we're doing happy hour on Friday. Let's unwind and have some girl talk about our lousy jobs. Want to come?"

Emma hesitated. "I'll check with my husband."

The conversation shifted to office gossip until Kelly giggled, "Just don't forget to wash your spoon with dish soap, or Derek will lose it. He's allergic to peanuts…EpiPen allergic."

Emma froze. "Peanut allergy?"

Jackie rolled her eyes. "Oh yeah. He treats dirty spoons like biohazards."

Emma's smile was thin. "Good to know."

When they left, she lingered by the microwave, watching the spoonful of peanut butter turn molten in a paper cup. She slipped it into her sleeve, her heartbeat steady, not fast. No guilt. No hesitation.

In Derek's office, she glanced toward the door before tilting the thick, amber liquid into his coffee. The empty cup went into the hallway trash can without a second thought.

She was halfway back to her desk when Derek rounded the corner.

"What were you doing in my office?" he asked.

"Getting the McGregor file," she said without missing a beat.

He studied her for a moment, then nodded and stepped inside.

Emma had just settled in when the sound hit, frantic, hacking coughs that escalated into shouts for an EpiPen. Footsteps pounded past her desk. She didn't turn, only listened as the commotion peaked: the jab into Derek's thigh, the gasping breaths, the relieved murmur when color returned to his face.

Minutes later, the break room filled with low voices and darting eyes. Emma leaned toward Carol, her tone laced with concern. "That was awful. Let me know if I can help while Derek recovers." Inside, a dark satisfaction curled warm in her chest.

The rest of the afternoon passed in a strange quiet. Without Derek barking orders, the office felt lighter, almost hushed…though Emma caught more than one coworker glancing her way. She kept her head down, pretending to work, already thinking about how much she hated this place. Derek's voice, Derek's rules, Derek's smug face, it wasn't worth her time.

By the time the clock neared three, she'd made up her mind. Today would be her last day. That afternoon, she picked Matt up from school. Ms. Francis met her at the door.

"I'm concerned about Ben," she said carefully. "He told kids he used to live in New York with his 'real mommy and daddy.'"

Emma's stomach knotted. "We lived with my sister and her husband before moving here after our apartment burned down. He's just confused."

"I see," Ms. Francis said, unconvinced.

Ms. Francis nodded, though her eyes stayed on Emma a moment longer than necessary.

In the car, Emma turned to Matt. "Remember what we talked about? We can't tell people about New York. They won't understand."

Matt crossed his arms. "But I want to go home."

Emma's grip on the wheel tightened. "This is your home. We love you. Please… try, okay?"

Matt stared out the window, saying nothing. The silence between them was heavier than the Florida heat.

In the kitchen that night, Andrés nursed a beer.

"Emma, we need to talk."

"About what?" she asked absently.

"About getting help. You're seeing things… talking to Jacob in your sleep. And now the school is asking questions. This can't go on."

Emma's eyes hardened. "You want to take him from me, too?"

"No. I want us to do the right thing."

"I am doing the right thing. He's my son now. We just celebrated his birthday two months ago."

"That's not how it works, Emma. That was Ben's birthday. He told you his birthday was in March."

Emma stepped closer. "You weren't there for Jacob. Or Carlos. Or Ben. Don't you dare try to take this from me."

Andrés looked at her, the full extent of her unraveling sinking in. "I think you need professional help."

Emma laughed bitterly. "I think you need to choose…us or your guilt."

Back in New York, Elena still visited the police station every day, clinging to hope, although it had been two years.

"Any updates?" she asked the officer at the front desk.

He shook his head. "I'm sorry."

Tears welled in her eyes. "It's his birthday today."

She wandered the streets, ending up at the neighborhood church. The empty pews echoed her footsteps as she walked to the front, where a crucifix hung above the altar.

"I don't understand, God. Why my baby?"

Behind her, Bishop Groover appeared silently. "You're not alone in your pain, Elena."

"I'm trying to stay strong, but I feel like I'm losing everything."

"In Hebrews 11:6 KJV, it says, 'But without faith it is impossible to please him...' Don't give up your faith."

"I want to believe he's alive. I feel it."

"Then trust that feeling. Come to our healing group on Thursday."

That night, Javier sat with his parents at home. A birthday cake sat in front of them.

"We will sing to Matt every year until he comes home," Javier said.

When Elena returned and saw the cake, she broke down. Javier wrapped his arms around her. "I can't let him go. He is six years old now."

They lit candles and prayed. Elena's voice trembled as she whispered, "Matt... we love you. Please come home."

And though the candles eventually burned out, the flame of her hope did not. Two years had passed since that Florida morning when Matt was just six.

Chapter 17
The Boy They Left Behind

While Emma clung to Matthew in Florida, locking doors, pulling blinds, shutting out questions far away in New York, another name from her past was about to surface. A name she thought she had erased.

But the past has a way of resurfacing.

It began two years earlier, when Carlos Diaz was just five years old, and the world forgot him.

It was a bitter spring morning, the kind that couldn't decide if it was winter or summer. The sky hung pale and cold over damp streets. On the side of his house, between two broken trash bins and a rusted-out grill, a little boy curled into himself beneath a thin blanket.

No shoes.

No jacket.

Only bruises and broken bones, hunger, and half-formed memories.

That's where Ms. Shirley Dawson found him. She was dragging her recycling out, muttering about the city's new bin rules, when she spotted a small bundle wedged near the cans. At first, she thought it was rags. Or maybe a stray cat.

Then it moved.

And whimpered.

"Lord Jesus," she breathed, dropping her bags.

She knelt. The boy's eyes fluttered open, brown, wide, glazed with fever. Blood speckled his shirt.

"What's your name, sweetheart?"

"Carlos," he whispered, lips dry and cracked.

She wrapped him in her coat, carried him inside, and felt the heat radiating off his skin. His breathing was shallow, each inhale fragile. Within the hour, she had him in the ER, signing intake papers as if he were her grandson. Carlos didn't correct her. He just stared at the scuffed linoleum.

Three days later, she walked him out of the hospital without looking back.

Shirley had lived next door to the Diaz family for years, a retired nurse in her fifties, still sharp and stubborn. She'd always suspected something was wrong in that house, too many fake smiles. Emma, especially, had a way about her.

A week after Carlos came home with Shirley, the Diaz house went dark. No lights. No voices. Gone.

Shirley didn't wait for explanations. She didn't call the police. Deep down, she knew: Carlos hadn't been lost. He'd been left. And she refused to see him swallowed by the system.

She packed her things, kissed the brick wall of her old house goodbye, and slipped out of town with Carlos like ghosts in the night.

They settled in a small two-bedroom apartment near the Cross Bronx Expressway. Shirley took a part-time job at a local clinic, enrolled Carlos in school under her last name, Carlos Dawson, and gave him what safety she could.

He was quiet at first. Jumpy. Afraid of bathtubs. But he clung to Shirley's hand like it was the only thing keeping him from vanishing.

When asked about his parents, Carlos would only say, "They got sad. And then they forgot me."

He remembered a staircase.

A bathtub.

A scream.

Then nothing.

Two years passed. By seven, Carlos was stronger—riding bikes, eating peanut butter sandwiches, sketching superheroes with crooked capes. His life with Ms. Shirley had begun to take root, steady and safe.

But in the quiet hours, the past still found him. Some nights, he woke in the hallway, tears streaking his face, whispering for the family who never came back.

"I'm still me," he'd whisper. "I'm still Carlos, right?"

"You are, baby," Shirley would say, stroking his curls. "You're still you. And you're still mine."

By the spring of that year, as Emma tried to keep Matthew's world small and hidden in Florida, Carlos's life in New York had quietly taken root, though the shadows of the past were never far behind.

Chapter 18
Growing Up Under the Sun

While Carlos's life quietly took root in New York, hidden beneath the watchful care of Ms. Shirley, Matthew's childhood unfolded under the relentless Florida sun.

Florida's summers were relentless, wrapping the days in heat so heavy it seemed to press the air right out of Matthew's lungs. By the time he turned six, he had learned to live in it, riding his bike down cracked sidewalks, racing the neighborhood kids, and coming home with grass stains on his shorts.

Life in Jacksonville looked normal enough to outsiders: school, a modest house, birthday cakes from the grocery store bakery. But inside, the rules were strict and unyielding. Emma kept a close watch, correcting his words, monitoring his friendships, and setting limits he didn't always understand. "We don't talk about before," she would say, her voice soft but final.

Matthew quickly learned that it was easier to follow the rules than to push against them; still, a quiet curiosity burned inside him, a desire to know more than he was allowed. School became Matthew's outlet, a place where the walls were farther apart, and the air felt freer.

By nine, his teachers began to notice his gift for numbers and problem-solving. Math came naturally to him, the logic fitting together like pieces of a puzzle he could see before anyone else. Science fascinated him, the why behind how things worked, from the stars above to the smallest cells under a microscope.

Emma encouraged his grades but discouraged independence. When a friend suggested they work together mowing lawns in the neighborhood, she refused. "You don't need a job," she told him. "Focus on school. Work is for adults."

By twelve, Matthew had his eyes set on becoming a doctor. The idea had taken root after a science lesson on the human body, and it grew with every biology book he checked out from the library. He could see himself in a white coat, listening to patients and solving the mysteries of the human body. It was a dream that made him feel larger than the life he lived.

His middle school years were filled with science club meetings, after-school study groups, and the occasional weekend trip to the library with his best friend, Lucas. Lucas shared his love of experiments, and the two often turned Matthew's small bedroom into a mini lab with beakers, vinegar, baking soda, and notebooks full of plans for bigger projects.

Emma didn't mind the experiments as long as they stayed inside and away from "bad influences." She never allowed him to attend sleepovers or go out without a reason she approved of. "The world is dangerous," she'd say, as if danger were always one open door away.

By fifteen, Matthew's reputation at school was clear: he was the kid who could tutor you in algebra, help you finish your lab report, and still find time to ace his work. He and Lucas began drafting ideas for a project that they both believed could win the regional science fair. Matthew's dream of becoming a doctor felt more reachable with each success, but there was a restless ache he couldn't shake. This was more than a project; it was a testament to the countless hours of study and the dream that had carried him for years.

Some nights, after finishing his homework, he'd sit on the back porch staring into the humid dark. He didn't know why, but it always felt like something, or someone, was out there beyond the fences and quiet streets.

He was only months away from turning sixteen, and with each passing day, the urge to break free from the boundaries Emma had built grew stronger.

While Matthew's teenage life moved forward in Florida, a forgotten past stirred quietly elsewhere.

Chapter 19
Traces of the Past

Back in New York, Detective Reagan sat alone in the precinct's evidence room, the hum of the overhead light buzzing like a persistent whisper. Before him lay a stack of manila folders, cases long considered cold, buried beneath newer tragedies.

One folder was different. This one held a fragment of the Diaz family's past, a piece he didn't know he needed until now.

Inside was the file for a toddler found inside a washing machine ten years ago. The file was thin: a brief autopsy report, estimated time of death, no fingerprints, no ID. The child had been labeled unidentified male.

Until now.

A recent citywide cold case initiative had pushed every forgotten file with viable evidence through the DNA database. This one had produced a match.

Ben Diaz.

Reagan's breath caught. "Ben Diaz…" he muttered, tapping his pen against the desk. The file referenced the old hospital records, the same ones that had haunted the case for years: three Diaz children. He stared at the names, each one a ghost from a broken family. One confirmed dead. One is now identified. And one is still missing.

The realization came like a tidal wave, drowning Reagan in memories, fragments of pain, and the haunting screams that had plagued his dreams for years, the day Emma and Andrés had left.

And now, sitting with the coroner's findings, he knew what had happened. Ben had drowned in the bathtub. Someone had hidden his body in the washing machine and fled.

Reagan closed the folder and stood. He and Lt. Chaser would have to notify the next of kin, but who were the Diazes' next of kin? Additional information was required, and further investigation was necessary.

A search through public records led them down a paper trail, including outdated driver's licenses, a marriage certificate, and an old utilities bill. One name kept resurfacing: Melissa Harper, Emma's older sister, last known to be living in a small town in New Jersey.

Two days later, they pulled up to a tired brick duplex with peeling paint and a crooked mailbox. It was late afternoon, the kind of gray day when shadows stretched long. Reagan felt the weight of the conversation they were about to have settle in his chest.

The door opened slowly. Melissa stood there, framed in the dim light of the hallway. She looked at them as if she'd already guessed who they were.

"She's not here," Melissa said before they even asked. Her voice was flat, but her fingers twisted the edge of her sweater. "I haven't seen Emma in over ten years."

Something in her tone carried more than distance; it had the sharp edge of old wounds.

They explained they were reopening an old case. Melissa sighed and leaned against the doorframe. "The last time I saw her, she showed up late at night. Said she'd been having dreams about having another child, like God was sending her a sign. I told her she needed therapy, but she laughed it off. She... she wasn't well.

She refused help, refused counseling. And when I asked about the boys, she avoided the question as if she were hiding something. Next thing I know… they were gone."

Her voice cracked. "She's not well; she needs help."

Reagan and Chaser exchanged a glance. They thanked Melissa for her time, took notes, and returned to the car, the weight of her words heavy between them.

As they were driving back to New York, Chaser's phone rang. The coroner's number flashed on the screen.

The voice on the other end was steady but heavy. Another DNA match. Another unidentified body.

But this one came with a name.

Elijah Gonzalez.

Emma had taken him from the mall to replace Ben, the child everyone believed was hers. The boy who had died near the park cliff the night she vanished.

The precinct launched a quiet but thorough investigation. Missing child reports from surrounding states were pulled until a match was found in New Jersey. Report read: Elijah had disappeared from a shopping mall eleven years ago. His mother, Isabela Gonzalez, had turned her back for less than a minute while paying at the counter. When she turned back, her son was gone.

For more than a decade, she had searched, distributing flyers, appearing on the news, and knocking on doors. She had refused to leave the neighborhood, clinging to hope that one day her son would be returned.

That day had finally come, though not in the way she had prayed for.

News of the DNA match traveled quickly, and so did the detectives. A two-hour drive brought Chaser and Reagan back to New Jersey, where a modest blue house with fading paint and flower beds waited at the end of the street. They stood on the front steps, the faded blue paint peeling beneath the porch light. Chaser lifted his hand and knocked, the sound echoing sharper than he intended.

A shuffle came from inside, then the rattle of a lock. The door opened, revealing a woman with weary eyes and deep lines etched by years of waiting.

"Mrs. Gonzalez?" Reagan asked softly, holding out his badge. "I'm Detective Reagan. This is Lt. Chaser. May we come in?

Isabela blinked rapidly, suspicion and cautious hope fighting for space in her eyes. "This is about Elijah?"

Reagan's voice softened. "Yes, ma'am. We have information to share with you and your husband. It's… It's not easy."

They sat in the living room, where a framed photo of a curly-haired toddler sat on the mantle, the same face Reagan had seen in the file.

Mateo's grip on Isabela's hand was tight enough to whiten his knuckles. "Please. Just tell us."

Reagan took a breath. "We've positively identified your son, Elijah. He passed away eleven years ago. He died in New York City."

Isabela let out a sound somewhere between a gasp and a sob.

"No. No, you must be wrong," Mateo whispered. "We checked New York. We filed reports. We never stopped looking."

"We believe he was abducted from the mall in New Jersey and taken to New York," Reagan explained. "He was raised under the name Ben Diaz. The couple who took him had lost a child of their own just days earlier, Ben Diaz drowned in a bathtub. In her state of trauma, the woman responsible, Emma Diaz, kidnapped Elijah and raised him as her son until he died in a tragic accident near a park cliff a year later."

Isabela covered her mouth, trembling. Lt. Chaser added gently, "We've recovered DNA samples confirming his identity, Elijah Gonzalez."

Elijah's parents sat motionless on the couch, clutching a wrinkled tissue. Her eyes were already red from days without rest; his jaw was clenched so tightly it looked painful to breathe. He didn't open the file in front of him. Instead, he closed his eyes...just for a second and let the memory take over.

"I wasn't there," Reagan said softly. "At the service. It was small. Quiet. A local childcare center, Blossoms and Bluebells Child Care Center, organized it. They didn't know his name yet, but they knew he mattered..."

"I was there," said Chaser.

Chaser's gaze drifted, letting the memory return.

The sky was a soft gray that morning, with low clouds and the gentle hush that often preceded rain. It was the kind of day that felt like a pause, like the world had stopped to listen.

A small group gathered beneath a white canopy at the edge of the cemetery. No news vans. No public officials. Just a few tearful staff from Blossoms and Bluebells, two daycare children holding flowers too big for their hands, and the funeral director who had waived his usual fee.

The tiny casket was white with silver trim. On top sat a single spray of bluebells and baby's breath, which was gentle, delicate, like the boy it represented.

Miss Denise, the center's director, stepped forward. Her voice trembled, but she held a paper in her hands. "We didn't know him," she said softly. "We didn't know his laugh, or his favorite snack, or the way he liked his blanket folded. But we know he mattered. We know someone loved him… and he should be remembered."

She paused, eyes wet. "He was buried under a name that wasn't truly his. But to us, he will always be remembered as a child of light. A child who should have had so many more days."

A little girl stepped forward, placing a crayon-drawn card against the casket. "Bye-bye, little one," she whispered.

Miss Denise stepped back, and a staff member pressed a small teddy bear next to the casket. No one spoke for a moment. Then came the soft murmur of "Amazing Grace," sung quietly by one of the teachers, shaky but pure. The others joined in, their voices rising like a lullaby meant to carry him to a better place. Tears spilled down Isabela's cheeks. Mateo pulled her close, resting his chin on her head. "We always knew. Somehow, we knew he wasn't just gone. Thank you for not letting him remain forgotten."

Reagan swallowed the lump in his throat. "I'm so sorry. I know it's not the outcome you were hoping for. But I promise you, your son mattered. He will never be just another case file."

They stayed a while longer, sharing memories and explaining next steps. Before leaving, Isabela handed Chaser a small photo. "This was his favorite. He was wearing his red sneakers. He said they made him run fast like a superhero."

Chaser accepted it with reverence.

Back in the car, Reagan looked over. "You okay?"

Chaser nodded slowly, though the weight of two lost boys...Matthew and Elijah sat heavily on his chest. "And I know what we have to do next."

"Matthew Colon?" Reagan asked.

"Yes," Chaser said. "There is still one more child out there. And I'm going to bring him home."

Back at the precinct, Lt. Chaser remembered that day vividly, not only for the sadness, though it had been heavy, but for the dignity. For the care taken by strangers who refused to let a nameless boy disappear without love.

And now, the headstone would read:

Elijah Gonzalez

Forever Loved. Never Forgotten.

1990-1995

Chapter 20
A Time to Heal

While Matthew's teenage years in Florida unfolded under watchful eyes, far away in New York, Elena's days were still marked by absence and unanswered prayers. The next morning, Elena lay in bed beside Javier, staring at the ceiling. Sunlight crept through the blinds, brushing her face with a warmth she could hardly feel.

"Are you mad at me?" she asked, her voice fragile.

Javier turned toward her. "Why would you think that?"

"Because I lost Matt the night of the fire, ten years ago. I never apologized for getting separated from him. I feel guilty every day, and I know you must be mad. He was our only child."

He reached for her hand. "I'm not mad at you. You were hurt. You couldn't get upstairs from the basement because your leg was broken. It wasn't your fault. And the most important thing is that Matt is alive. I believe that. The couple who took him may have lost a child and replaced him with ours. But I pray every day that Matt remembers us and finds his way back."

Javier's voice thinned under the weight of tears. "I walk through the park every day on my way to work, hoping to see him playing. I want to hate the people who took him, but I can't live in anger. It's not healthy. For me. For you. For us. I love you, Elena. We have to stick together for Matt."

Elena's lip trembled. "It's hard. I'm at the police station every day searching for answers. Some days... I want it to end."

Javier sat up, gripping her shoulders gently. "Don't say that. Please. You're stronger than you think. We can't give up. His case may be cold, but that doesn't mean we stop hoping."

She nodded slowly. "I promise. I saw Bishop Groover yesterday. He invited us to the healing class again this Thursday night."

"We'll go," Javier said. "Let's lean on our church and community. Let's keep our faith." He kissed her forehead. "Stay in bed. I'll make breakfast."

As Javier left the room, Elena listened to his footsteps fade down the hall. She closed her eyes, whispering a prayer into the quiet, one more plea that somewhere, somehow, Matt would hear her. Elena watched him leave the room and sank deeper into the pillows.

"I can do this," she whispered into the quiet. "Just believe in God. He will get us through. I believe."

Thirty minutes later, Javier returned with a tray of breakfast: fluffy scrambled eggs, golden toast, crisp bacon, and a bowl of fresh peaches glistening with juice. The scent filled the room, warm and comforting. Elena smiled through grateful tears.

"You're not mad at me?" she asked, her voice softer this time, almost teasing.

"Never," Javier said, brushing a stray lock of hair from her face. "We'll get through this. Together."

As she ate, he set a glossy travel brochure on her lap.

"Let's take a vacation."

Her brows lifted. "A vacation? Where would we even go?"

"The Bahamas. A week in the sun. It might help you clear your mind."

Elena hesitated, her fingers stilling on the edge of the blanket. She searched his face, trying to read the reason behind his sudden suggestion. "Do we even have the money for that?"

Javier's smile deepened, though there was a trace of hope in his eyes. "Yes, we do." He reached over, opened the bedside drawer, and pulled out two airline tickets, the paper crisp between his fingers.

Elena's eyes widened. Her breath caught, and for a moment she forgot to blink. "Oh, my goodness! Why didn't you tell me you already had the trip planned?"

"I wanted it to be a surprise," he said softly, as if the trip was more than just a getaway, maybe a chance to bring them back to something they'd lost.

She set her plate aside and leaned into his chest. "You always think ahead."

"That's what husbands do."

They stayed like that for a moment, letting the idea of tomorrow sink in. Elena's thoughts drifted to the ocean, its rhythm, its calm, and she felt a strange lightness in her chest.

By evening, their suitcases lay open across the bed, clothes folded into neat stacks. The thought of turquoise water, white sand, and quiet evenings wrapped around her like a warm blanket. For the first time in years, she felt a glimmer of anticipation instead of dread.

The following morning, they boarded the plane. Elena sat by the window, watching the world fall away beneath them. Sunlight poured through the clouds in ribbons, and Javier reached for her hand.

"We're going to be okay," he said.

She turned to him. "I want to heal, Javier. I want to live again." And for the first time since the fire, she truly meant it.

The Bahamas Resort and Spa was a postcard brought to life…palm trees swaying in the salt breeze, waves whispering against the shore, and air scented faintly with coconut and hibiscus. Elena and Javier spent their days walking barefoot along the beach, reading by the pool, and talking, honestly talking for the first time in years. They laughed over candlelit dinners, sipped chilled coconut drinks, and watched the sunrise from their balcony, the horizon painted in shades of coral and gold. But even in paradise, Matt was never far from their thoughts.

One evening, swaying gently in a hammock beneath a silver-bright full moon, Elena's voice broke the quiet.

"Do you think he remembers us?"

Javier's gaze stayed on the night sky. "I think the heart remembers what the mind forgets. Wherever he is, I believe he feels our love."

Elena brushed away a tear. "Then let's keep sending it until he finds his way home."

By the end of the week, Elena was steadier. She had laughed. She had cried. But she had not broken.

As their plane dipped back toward the city skyline, she laced her fingers through Javier's. They had stepped away from grief for a moment, but now they would face it again, together, anchored by faith.

Two days after returning home, the phone on the kitchen wall rang, its shrill tone echoing through the house. Javier reached for the receiver, the cord twisting as he lifted it to his ear.

"I have cancer," his mother said. Vera didn't waste any time with small talk. Her voice was steady, but underneath it, Javier heard the tremor she tried to hide. She told him not to worry about the illness, only that she needed to see Chico before she died. The call ended with her promise to hold on as long as she could.

Javier sat at the kitchen table, hands covering his mouth. Elena joined him, her heart tightening as she saw the weight in his eyes. He told her everything, voice breaking as he whispered,

"Matthew... come home."

Elena reached for his hands, holding them firmly in hers. "We'll find a way," she said, her voice quiet but confident. She didn't know how, but she meant it.

Because Matt was still out there.

And home was waiting.

Far away, in another house, one that was not bound by love, Matt was waking to a very different morning. By the time he turned sixteen, the walls around his life in Florida had begun to crack, not in brick or wood, but in truth.

Chapter 21
A Mind of His Own

Now, Sixteen-year-old Matt cracked his eyes open. He hated early mornings, but school was different; it was the only place he felt like himself. A space where "Ben" existed only on attendance sheets. A space where he could lose himself in logic, technology, and innovation. Science was his sanctuary.

Today was special. The 10th-grade science and medical fair. He'd been working for months on a cardiogenic device designed to detect heart irregularities before symptoms appeared. This wasn't just a school project; it was the first step toward his dream of becoming a cardiologist.

"I'm ready! I've been up since six," he said, bounding down the stairs. "The science fair's this afternoon. I'm presenting my instrument to detect potential heart attacks before they happen."

"We are so proud of you," Andrés said, sipping his coffee with a warm smile. "You're going to make a brilliant doctor."

Eleven years had passed since he was taken. Florida had become the backdrop of his childhood, but Matt had never forgotten the truth. He wasn't from here. He wasn't Ben Diaz. And these weren't his parents.

Some memories clung stubbornly: the corner store across from their apartment, snow collecting on fire escapes, the Statue of Liberty glowing under a pink dusk sky. He remembered his birth father lifting him onto his shoulders to see her better.

But his last name? Gone. Only his first name, Matthew, remained.

That name had resurfaced in preschool, and the fallout had been swift. He'd told a teacher he wasn't from Florida, and Emma had pulled him out of school for two weeks. After that, she began volunteering at his private school, shadowing him through hallways and class parties. She quit working altogether, her watchful presence growing into paranoia.

Despite the tension at home, Matt thrived academically. His world was small but steady, anchored by his best friend, Lucas. Together, they had poured months into their science project, each late-night tweak and adjustment bringing them closer to this moment.

As they stepped into the gym that morning, Lucas's expression tightened.

"We need at least twenty minutes to set up the prototype. Plus, we have to combine tables. Let's move!"

"Relax," Matt said with a smirk. "We've got this."

Before they could reach their station, Brian from the football team blocked their path.

"Where are the nerds rushing off to?"

"We've got actual work to do," Lucas shot back. "So, unless you're entering a protein shake in the fair, move."

Brian's eyes narrowed, and he stepped closer. "What did you just say?"

Before the tension could snap, Mr. Bryant's voice cut in.

"Brian, office. Now. You're already on bullying notice, and I'm not in the mood."

Brian muttered something under his breath but backed away.

"Thanks, Mr. Bryant," Matt said.

"Go win the fair, boys," the teacher replied with a nod.

They got to work. Lucas grinned as he unpacked wires and monitors.

"Today's the day. I'm wearing my lucky black-and-green zebra socks. Guaranteed win."

Matt froze. "What did you just say?"

"My zebra socks. Why?"

Matt's gaze fixed on them.

"You okay?" Lucas asked.

"Yeah… I just remembered something. I had a jacket with that pattern. The day everything changed."

Lucas's hands slowed. "What happened?"

Matt hesitated, then spoke quietly. "They're not my parents. Emma and Andrés. I don't know how I ended up with them, but I remember New York. I remember my real parents."

Lucas nodded slowly. "I'm sorry, man. I didn't know."

"I want to find them," Matt said. "I just don't know how."

"Maybe we can figure it out," Lucas said. "Together."

For the first time, Matt felt like the search wasn't his burden alone.

"Yeah, keep this between you and me."

"You got it," said Lucas.

The science fair buzzed with excitement. Judges moved from booth to booth, clipboards in hand. Projects lined the gym walls, each one a piece of someone's dream.

"Please, quiet down," Principal Jensen's voice echoed. "The judges have chosen the top three projects."

Students pressed toward the stage.

"Third place," she announced, "Meghan and Connor, for their ultra-beam dental microscope."

Polite clapping.

"Second place: Thomas and Leah, for their freeze-dry meat container."

"And now," said Frederick Evans, visiting Nobel Prize winner, "First place goes to… Matt and Lucas for their cardiogenic diagnostic device!"

Cheers erupted. Lucas whooped. "Told you. My socks!"

Matt managed a smile, but his thoughts were elsewhere.

When Mr. Evans approached them afterward and encouraged them to apply to the top medical program in New York, Matt's heart skipped a beat.

"New York," he whispered. The name felt like a key turning in a long-locked door.

A few weeks later, a storm broke loose in Emma's mind.

It started the moment she burst into school unannounced.

Matt had just finished lunch when shouts echoed down the hallway.

"WHERE IS MY SON?!"

Students froze mid-step. Teachers rushed toward the noise.

Emma appeared suddenly, barefoot, the slap of her feet on the tile sharp and startling, blouse inside out, hair disheveled, eyes wild.

Matt's stomach dropped.

She spotted him instantly.

"Ben! BEN! They're trying to take you from me!"

"Mom, calm down!" Matt said, backing away.

She slapped a tray off the nearest table. Food splattered to the floor.

"Don't you dare talk to me like I'm crazy! I raised you! You're MINE!"

Security arrived. Emma kicked, screamed, and clawed at their arms as they restrained her.

Matt stood frozen, heat crawling up his neck. Lucas slipped in beside him, wide-eyed.

"I'm sorry," Matt whispered. "She wasn't always like this."

"You okay?" Lucas asked quietly.

"No." Matt's voice was tight. "But I will be."

That night, Andrés sat across from him at the kitchen table.

"She stopped taking her meds," he said heavily. "When she feels threatened, the episodes come." Andres lied. Emma never began treatment to address her mental health.

Matt didn't answer. He'd already stopped listening; it was easier than hearing the same excuses over and over. Upstairs, he opened his laptop and pulled up a missing child database.

Male. Age 4. Missing. New York. 12 years ago.

Page after page of cases scrolled by.

Then he saw it.

Matthew C.

No photo. Just a name. But it felt like his. He closed the tab and reached for his journal.

Dear Mom and Dad,

I think I'm closer to finding you. I still don't know my last name, but I know I'm not Ben. I'm not theirs. I remember the Statue of Liberty. I remember love. Real love. I won't stop looking. I promise.

Love, Matthew

Chapter 22
Whispers in the City

Only a few weeks had passed since Matt and Lucas stood on stage with their first-place ribbon, but the science fair already felt like a doorway to something bigger, something that might finally lead him home.

After the science fair, Lucas and Matthew met with Principal Jensen and Mr. Evans.

"At the beginning of your senior year, I would like to invite you and your parents to tour our department," Mr. Evans said warmly. "Principal Jensen will explain all of the details, but here's an overview of the program."

Matt thanked him, trying to contain his excitement. Lucas practically bounced beside him.

Principal Jensen stepped forward. "We'll reach out to each student's parents with program details and potential scholarship opportunities. Excellent work, now head to the fifth period."

Matt walked through the halls in a daze, clutching his ribbon and trophy.

This is my chance, he thought. An opportunity to go back to New York... maybe even find them.

But even as the thought sparked hope, a shadow followed: Andres and Emma would have to approve. And Andres never told Emma anything that might upset her. Not the truth. Not the whole story.

He gently tapped the side of his head, reflecting thoughtfully. Senior year... one last chance to find out who I really am.

"Why are you hitting your head, Matt?" Lucas asked, coming up behind him. "You okay, man? Ever since the sock thing, you've been acting weird."

Matt gave a half-hearted smile. "Yeah, yeah. I'm fine. Let's get to class."

But inside, he wasn't fine. The idea of going to New York wasn't just exciting; it was a lifeline, a chance to go home.

After school, Matt stood by the entrance, nervously gripping an envelope. When Andrés pulled up, Matt hopped into the car with a grin.

"Remember the science fair a few weeks ago?" he said, sliding into the passenger seat. He held up the letter. "They just sent this, an official invitation to visit one of the top medical schools in New York at the very start of my senior year!"

Andrés's expression stiffened. "Oh."

Matt nodded. "Yeah, it's for three days. Principal Jensen will call or email. It's a big deal."

Andres's grip tightened on the steering wheel. He forced a smile. "That's... great. Let's talk to your mom about it."

Inside the house, Matt rushed to show Emma the letter.

"I'm so happy for you, baby," Emma said, squeezing him tight.

"And he's going to New York his senior year for a science trip," Andres added, keeping his tone casual but watching her closely.

Emma froze. Her eyes widened, and her expression darkened. Her lips trembled before she forced the word out.

"Not."

Matt's smile dropped. "What? Why?"

Emma said nothing, her face pale. The guilt was plain, but she did not explain.

"What's wrong?" Matt pressed.

Andres stepped in quickly, voice calm but calculated, the same voice he used when hiding things. "Your mom's just surprised. We'll figure things out with the school."

Matt never liked the word mom. He never liked saying it, never liked hearing it. They weren't his parents, and deep down, he knew they never had been.

Later, lying on his bed, he thought about Emma's face when she heard New York. There was something there, something she didn't want him to find.

"They're hiding something," he whispered. "But what?"

He reached under his mattress and pulled out his journal. That night, he wrote another entry:

Dear Mom and Dad,

I got a letter today. They want me to visit a medical school in New York during my senior year. I don't know if I'll get to go, but if I do... maybe I'll find you. I hope you're still looking for me.

The end of sophomore year bled into junior year, a blur of late-night exams, lab work, and weekend hours with Lucas, building prototypes and researching scholarships. The New York trip stayed far on the horizon, but it was always in the back of Matt's mind.

Emma kept him close. Too close.

Lucas came by most weekends, lugging his backpack full of wires, circuit boards, and half-finished projects. The two boys spent hours at the kitchen table, building and testing small prototypes, while Emma moved about the house, dusting shelves that didn't need dusting, refilling water glasses before they were half empty.

"You boys okay in here?" she'd ask every twenty minutes, her tone casual but her eyes sharp.

"We're fine, Mom," Matt would answer, never looking up from his soldering iron.

Emma never let him go to Lucas's house. "It's not personal," she'd say. "I just like knowing you're safe."

Safe. Matt had learned that words didn't always mean what they should.

Sometimes, he'd catch her standing in the doorway, watching him work, her arms folded tightly as if she were holding herself together. If Lucas noticed, he didn't say anything. But once, when Emma stepped out to check the mail, Lucas muttered, "Dude… she's intense."

"Yeah," Matt replied, forcing a smile. "You get used to it."

Summer came and went, and senior year crept closer.

As August drew near, the invitations for the senior-year science tour to New York began arriving. Principal Jensen called to confirm the trip dates: early fall. Matt's chest tightened with excitement, but he kept his voice even on the phone.

Emma listened from the kitchen. She didn't say a word.

That night, Matt wrote in his journal:

Dear Mom and Dad,

Senior year starts soon. I think I'm getting closer.

He tucked the notebook back under his mattress before turning off the light.

Down the hall, Emma lay awake, staring at the ceiling. She told herself she was just being protective. But deep down, she knew the truth: Matthew was slipping out of her grasp.

And she wasn't sure she could stop it. He marked the days on his calendar, each red X a small victory. By late August, the air in Florida still clung heavily and humidly, but senior year was about to begin. One step closer to New York. One step closer to the truth.

The first week of school passed in a blur of schedules, assignments, and polite congratulations about the science fair win. Matt could barely focus on any of it. The trip to New York was scheduled for the end of September, and he kept the permission slip in his backpack as if it were a golden ticket. Emma remained tense in the weeks leading up to the trip. She insisted on packing his suitcase herself, refolding shirts he had already folded, double-checking the zipper, and tucking an emergency cash envelope in the side pocket.

"Stick with your dad at all times," she warned for the third time that week. "New York is big and dangerous."

"I will," Matt said, though his eyes told a different story. He had no intention of sticking by Andres every moment.

The morning of the flight arrived. Inside the terminal, they met up with Lucas, his father, and Mr. Groosemen, who was chaperoning the trip. Emma had stayed home, claiming she wasn't feeling well. Matt suspected the real reason was that she couldn't bear to watch him walk through that gate.

The flight to New York was smooth. Matt sat by the window, eyes fixed on the clouds, heart racing faster with each mile north. When the city skyline came into view, something inside him stirred.

At baggage claim, he felt an odd rush of familiarity. The smells, the sounds, the chaos, it was as if he had stepped into a place both strange and known. He couldn't explain it to Andres, so he didn't try.

In the cab to their hotel, Matt pressed his forehead against the glass, searching every street corner for something, anything, that might pull another memory to the surface.

This was more than a science trip. This was a homecoming he couldn't yet prove.

Mr. Groosemen, their science teacher, handed out room keys in the lobby. "Dinner's at six, business casual. Tomorrow is the full campus tour."

Matt's heart sank when he saw his assignment: sharing a room with Andres. Across the lobby, Lucas grinned, holding a key next to his father.

Inside the room, Andres unpacked neatly, his every movement deliberate. Matt stayed by the window, staring out at the skyline.

"This place feels like home," he murmured.

Andres looked up from his suitcase. "Home is Florida," he said flatly. "Don't forget that."

Matt didn't answer.

Dinner was lively, the air buzzing with ambition. Students from across the country swapped stories of scholarships, internships, and big plans. Afterward, Mr. Evans pulled Matt aside.

"You're a talented young man," he said. "I see future greatness in you. Keep this momentum. Apply early."

"I will, sir. Thank you."

The next day, during a break in the campus tour, Matt slipped away. He followed a garden path until he reached the sidewalk, eyes scanning the blocks. Then, he froze.

Across the street stood a miniature replica of the Statue of Liberty in front of a souvenir shop.

A flicker of memory rushed in, his father's shoulders beneath him, the smell of saltwater, a voice saying, See that, Matt? That's freedom.

He gripped the strap of his backpack.

"I remember," he whispered.

That night, in the dim hotel room, Andres was already asleep. Matt lay on his back, staring at the ceiling, the memory replaying over and over. Eventually, he slipped quietly into the hall, careful not to wake him.

The precinct was only a few blocks away. His pulse pounded as he stepped inside.

"Can I help you?" the officer at the front desk asked.

"I... I think I was abducted as a child," Matt said quietly. "I want to file a report. My name is Matthew. I don't know my last name. I was taken from here when I was four."

The officer's brow furrowed. "Do you have proof?"

Matt hesitated. "No, but…"

"Kid, unless there's evidence or someone's actively missing you, there's not much we can do. Go home."

Matt's chest tightened. He turned without another word, stepping back into the night. The city lights still burned bright…but the truth felt farther away than ever.

Chapter 23
Last Night

The day after leaving the precinct, he was devastated that he hadn't been able to tell his story. Lost in thought as he quietly walked through the lobby, he noticed the final session of the science conference at the medical school ending in polite applause and tired smiles.

Attendees stood as chairs scraped slowly, shouldering canvas tote bags stuffed with glossy brochures, lanyards, and last-minute business cards.

The air smelled like lukewarm coffee and carpet cleaner; the microphone squealed once and died.

Andres clapped Matt on the back, beaming. "You managed yourself well," he said. "That presentation on synthetic tissue growth? You nailed it."

Matt forced a small smile. "Thanks."

They were flying back to Florida in the morning. Part of him was relieved, the weight of the trip, the sting of the precinct's dismissal, the late-night hours replaying every word, clung to him like a second skin.

But the other part felt unfinished. Like the city was a room he'd been in once as a child, lights off, and if he could find the switch...

"You sure you're okay?" Andres asked, slowing with him on the stone steps outside the lecture hall.

"Just tired," Matt said.

But he wasn't tired.

He was waiting.

For something. For someone. For the truth to finally have a face.

They crossed the courtyard with the others, a murmuring river of students and teachers drifting toward the gates.
Matt kept a half-step behind Andres, staring past the heads of the crowd to the twilight skyline, where windows burned like a thousand tiny beacons.

Back at the hotel, the conference trickled into the mezzanine lounge. Voices rose and dimmed in pockets: congratulations, a small argument over a paper citation, a burst of laughter that hit Matt like static.
He stood at the window for a moment, breathing. In the glass, he saw himself faintly tall, older than he felt, eyes too alert to be called tired.

"Earth to Matt." Lucas nudged him with an elbow and held up two paper cups. "Victory caffeine?"

Matt took one. "Thanks."

They sat near the railing, the lobby below them a slow carousel of luggage carts and revolving doors.
Mr. Groosemen waved from the elevators and mouthed, "Curfew at ten." Lucas grinned, mouthed back, "We're angels."

Matt wrapped both hands around his cup and let the heat sting his palms.
The scratch of the conference pen on the sign-in sheet earlier had sounded like the pen at the precinct, his name on the line, his voice steady, the officer's face a wall.
Go home, the man had said, and the words had dug in like grit.

The elevator chimed. A family stepped out, a little boy on a father's shoulders, the mother balancing a stack of room keys and a bag of snacks.

The boy's laugh rolled up through the atrium, bright, unquestioning. Matt's chest tightened, a simple ache with no place to go.

"You're doing that thing," Lucas said softly, not looking at him. "Where you watch the world like it's going to tell you a secret."

"Maybe it will."

They sipped in silence.

"Tomorrow we fly," Lucas said eventually. "You'll ace the fall apps. We'll get back for homecoming, you'll do your cardiology shadowing, your life will be aggressively normal."

Matt huffed. "That's supposed to be comforting?"

"Kinda." Lucas slouched. "Also, I'm not good at feelings."

"You're not terrible," Matt said. He set the cup on the table and then stood. "I'm going to walk the lobby. Five minutes."

Lucas nodded, already digging in his tote for the session notes he'd promised to reorganize for the team. "I'll be here."

Matt took the stairs down instead of the elevator, hand sliding along the cool brass rail.

The lobby glowed with lamps like minor planets, the air scented faintly with polished wood. The desk clerk flipped a page in a ledger, the slow hush of doors opening and closing filling the space.

A delivery cart rolled in from the entrance, stacked boxes and a clipboard balanced on top. Behind it, a man in a windbreaker pushed steadily toward the front desk. He spoke briefly with the clerk, sliding the clipboard toward her for a signature.

Matt crossed the marble floor, glancing toward the desk out of habit, and met the man's eyes.

The moment caught them both. Something in the set of the jaw, the shape of the eyes, the weight of the gaze felt like a memory too distant to name. Neither spoke. Neither smiled. But neither looked away right away, either.

The clerk handed back the clipboard. The man gave a short nod and turned toward the door, pushing the cart out into the afternoon air.

Matt stood for a second longer, palm against the back of his neck. Then he headed for the stairs, the echo of that look lingering in his mind.

Outside, Javier steered the cart toward his truck, but his thoughts stayed behind — on the boy in the lobby with the familiar eyes, and a feeling he couldn't shake.
Matt blinked, ran a palm over the back of his neck, and went back up the stairs.

Andres was waiting by the elevators, jacket folded over his arm, the pleasant, practiced smile of a man at the end of a long day. "Early flight," he said. "We should pack."

"In a minute," Matt said. "I'll, uh, help Lucas finish his notes."

"Don't be long."

Matt crossed the mezzanine toward the conference banners. He didn't look back.

Across town, a white box truck eased through traffic, the radio turned low to a station that only played the old songs after nine. Javier Colon drove with the collar of his windbreaker unzipped, one wrist resting on the wheel, the other hand flattening the delivery manifest uselessly on the passenger seat, smoothing creases that didn't matter.

He'd already left the hotel hours ago. He'd already completed six stops since then.
He'd eaten half a sandwich in a loading bay and thrown the other half away without tasting it.
Between Sixth and Seventh, a man in a suit had cut off his truck, and he hadn't even sworn, and the day had moved on. He had not.

That face.

Those eyes.

The way the boy stood weight pitched slightly forward, a habit picked up from years of reaching for something taller to see better.

"Coincidence," he said aloud to no one. His voice startled him. He cleared his throat and signaled right.

He tried to think about practical things: the 7:00 drop off on the West End, the signature he needed from a superintendent who hated signing, the parking ticket he was going to get if he stopped on the hydrant again.
He tried not to think about Elena. He tried not to think about the way hope could cut a person open if you held it wrong.

The light turned red at 86th. He braked, yielded to a group in the crosswalk: a father carrying a pink backpack, a little girl skipping, a woman pushing a stroller with a sleeping baby whose hair stuck up in an impossible swirl.

A memory rose uninvited of Matthew at four, post-nap, hair at every angle, asking, "Is the lady torch heavy? In that way, kids could ask a question so simple it could change the way you saw the whole world.

Javier gripped the wheel and let the memory pass through him like a wave.

The light went green. He didn't move right away. A horn tapped, impatient but not cruel. He rolled forward.

He almost turned back to the hotel twice, once at a corner where he could have made the U, once when a spot opened right in front of the loading zone, like the city itself was offering him a door. He didn't.

He drove on, past the places he knew and the places he'd rather forget, route lines matching the map he'd drawn in his head so often it felt tattooed there.

He didn't call Elena. He thought about it, thumb hovering over her name on the screen while he idled in a double-park, but he couldn't make himself say the words I saw a boy and for a second I thought...

Not when he had no right to raise that hope and not enough courage to name the fear beneath it.

At the next light, he glanced in the rearview mirror. For a ridiculous instant, he expected to see the boy in the road behind him, walking toward the truck with that same steady, searching look.

Empty street. Pedestrians. A courier balancing two coffee trays with alarming grace.

"Nothing," he said, and eased forward.

Evening draped itself over the hotel like a calm hand.

On the mezzanine, Matt and Lucas sat surrounded by a low wall of session folders and neon sticky notes, the conference's last chaos spread in patient rows.

Lucas had color-coded half their week; Matt had pretended to help and mostly stared past his friend's shoulder at the slow choreography of the lobby below.

"You want yellow for action items or green?" Lucas asked, pen between his teeth.

"Green," Matt said, without looking. "No, yellow. I don't care."

"Earth-shattering decisiveness," Lucas said dryly. He set the pen down and leaned back. "Okay, talk to me. Not to fix it. To say it out loud."

Matt dragged a hand through his hair. He pictured the precinct, the cool tile under his feet, the steady hum of the fluorescent lights, the officer's eyes kind but already drifting away.

Unless there's evidence… go home.

His mind shifted to the lobby. Moments earlier, it had felt completely ordinary until it didn't. Something had changed. It was as if a feeling had walked in wearing a stranger's face, tapping him on the shoulder, whispering, Pay attention.

"Do you ever… know something," he asked slowly, "and also not know it at all?"

"All the time," Lucas said. "It's called physics."

Matt cracked a reluctant smile.

"Look," Lucas went on, softer. "Whatever it is, you're not crazy."

"I know."

"You'll find them."

Matt nodded, though the nod felt like a promise he had no way to keep.
He reached for his notebook, thumb smoothing the dog-eared corner where his first letter lived.
Dear Mom and Dad... He didn't open it. He didn't need the words tonight; he needed the horizon of them.

Mr. Groosemen appeared at the edge of the mezzanine, checked his watch, and pointed at his own eyes in the universal "I'm watching you" sign.
Lucas saluted. Matt lifted his hand.

"Ten," Lucas said. "We should pack."

"Yeah."

They tidied the stacks. Lucas stuffed the last of the notes into his tote.
They stood, shouldered their bags, and drifted toward the elevators with the last stragglers from the conference.

The doors slid open; the car filled; the doors slid shut.

Matt watched the floor numbers on the elevator wall climb. At nine, he caught his reflection in the brushed steel, older and younger at once.

At ten, he looked down at his shoes. At eleven, he lifted his chin and decided that tomorrow, when the plane rose over the water and the city shrank, he would look back only once.

Across town, Javier eased the truck into its bay at the delivery hub, the engine ticking in the cooling night air. The lot was mostly empty now, just a few other drivers finishing their paperwork under the glare of floodlights.

He cut the engine, sat for a moment in the cab, and let the quiet settle.

He could still go back, he thought. Even now. No rule said you had to let a thing go just because it was scary to hold.

He imagined walking into that hotel lobby again, asking the desk clerk if a young man with dark hair was staying there with a school group. Imagined the clerk tilting her head and saying, "Which one?" And the whole idea is collapsing like a house of cards.

With a sigh, he stepped down from the truck, dropped the last clipboard on the counter inside, and signed out for the night.

Work first. Questions later. It was the only way he knew to keep moving.

Still, as he walked across the lot toward his car, keys in hand, he felt the weight of a thread, thin, invisible, stretched from somewhere in his chest to somewhere in the city he could not name.

He didn't tug it. He didn't cut it. He just breathed around it, unlocked the car, and drove into the night.

In the hotel room, Andres folded shirts with careful, tidy hands, zippers sighing shut. "Alarm at five," he said, not looking up. "We'll beat the morning rush."

"Okay," Matt said.

He lay on his back and watched light crawl along the ceiling, stripes from the streetlamps carving the dark into even pieces.

He counted the silence between car horns. He counted the breaths until his chest stopped feeling like a fist.

He closed his eyes.

New York remained. It did not respond. However, it persisted.

And somewhere beyond the window, a sedan rolled through a green light, its driver glancing once toward the hotel before turning east toward the bridge.

And somewhere below, a man stepped through a revolving door and did not turn back.

And somewhere inside himself, a boy who had once been four touched a memory by its edges and did not let it slip away this time.

Tomorrow they would fly. Tonight, he waited.

Javier drove through the thinning traffic, the muted glow of the dashboard painting his hands in pale light. The day was over; the truck was parked, and the last signature had been logged hours ago. But the image of the boy in the hotel lobby stayed with him, replaying each time he blinked.

Could it have been Matthew?

The question rode with him the rest of the way home.

He didn't tell Elena right away. But the next morning, unable to let it go, he confessed over breakfast. Her coffee cup rattled in its saucer.

"We have to go back," she said, already grabbing her purse.

They drove to the hotel near the university, hope tightening in their chests. At the front desk, Javier leaned forward.

"I was here yesterday delivering packages. There was a science conference for high school students. I think our son may have been here; he's been missing for fourteen years."

The clerk's expression softened. "I'm so sorry. An outside agency hosted that event. All reservations were under the attending adults' names. We've already cleared most of this week's records for a system reset."

"Please," Elena urged, her voice breaking. "Someone must have seen him. He would've been with a man, maybe a teacher."

The clerk hesitated. "I can take your contact information. If anyone remembers, I'll reach out."

They left with nothing but a folded slip of paper and the weight of another missed chance.
As they walked to the car, Elena clutched Javier's arm.

"I really thought we'd find something."

Javier didn't answer right away. The city noise swirled around them like car horns, footsteps, the rush of someone else's life moving forward.

Finally, he looked at her. His voice was low, steady, but it trembled at the edges.

"We almost did."

He swallowed hard, the words like stones in his mouth. "And almost…" He shook his head, breath catching. "…almost is worse than nothing."

They stood there a moment longer, two people holding onto hope, but it's so sharp it could cut them open. Somewhere out there, the boy they'd been chasing for fourteen years was close enough to touch, and just far enough to lose again.

Chapter 24
The Glimpse

Back in Florida, the afternoon sun spilled across Matt's room as he unpacked the last of his bags from the science trip. But even surrounded by laundry and textbooks, his mind wasn't here; it was still in that hotel lobby. The glance had lasted only seconds, yet something in that man's eyes... a flicker of recognition he couldn't shake.

That evening, Lucas came over for dinner, eager to rehash the trip. Emma fussed over the boys, piling their plates high while Andres lingered in the kitchen doorway, silent as ever.

"You've got to get a date early, man," Lucas teased between bites. "Don't wait until the week of like last year."

Matt gave a distracted half-smile, swirling his drink. "Yeah. We'll see."

Lucas tilted his head. "What's up with you? You've been quiet since yesterday."

Just tired." It was easier than explaining that those eyes didn't just seem familiar; his eyes felt like a part of him. The weekend passed in its usual quiet, and by Monday morning, school routines had resumed. The last weeks of senior year blurred past. Homecoming came and went, Lucas in a deep blue suit, Matt in a charcoal one, both trying to look relaxed for the photos. Matt danced, laughed, and even smiled for Emma's camera. But in the quiet moments, the image from the lobby still pressed against his thoughts.

Prom arrived in the spring, the Florida heat settling in early. Matt stood in the driveway while Emma fussed over his tie, snapping picture after picture. Andres leaned on the porch rail, clapping him on the shoulder. "Enjoy tonight," he said with a small smile. But Matt could see the guilt flicker in his eyes.

Graduation day was sweltering. Rows of caps and gowns shimmered in the sun as families crowded the bleachers. Emma stood in the front row, ready with her camera before Matt's name was even called. "This is my day too," she whispered to Andres, pride brimming in her voice, edged with something sharper as though she'd claimed a prize no one could take away.

Andres clapped when Matt crossed the stage, but it was measured, his gaze low.

After the ceremony, Emma pulled Matt into photo after photo, wrapping her arms around him with a possessiveness that made onlookers smile. Still, if anyone looked closer, they might have seen the ownership in her grip. To her, every milestone Matt reached was hers to claim.

Matt posed with friends, accepted gifts, and smiled on cue, but inside, the restlessness deepened. The day felt incomplete as if someone who mattered were missing from the crowd.

College move-in day came that August. Matt unpacked boxes in his small dorm room while Emma directed from the doorway. "Don't hang that there, it'll block the light. Eat breakfast every morning. Call me every Sunday." Her voice was syrupy with care, but each word carried the weight of control.

Andres lingered in the hallway. When Matt set a faded crayon drawing of the Statue of Liberty on his desk, Andres froze.

"Where'd you get that?"

Matt shrugged. "Had it forever. Must've drawn it when I was a kid."

Later that night, lying in bed, Matt traced the outline of the statue's torch with his finger. He couldn't remember drawing it…only that it felt like remembering something he wasn't supposed to.

The years that followed were a blur of exams, lab experiments, and late-night projects with Lucas. College came fast and harder study lectures that ran past dusk, internships in bustling hospitals, and friendships built over vending machine coffee. But no matter how busy life became, every so often, a city skyline or a stranger's face would stir something in him, the way that old drawing had.

On a bright spring morning in Massachusetts, Matt stood in a black cap and gown, waiting with Lucas at the edge of the quad.

"Graduation day, man. We actually made it," Lucas grinned.

"And medical school is next," Matt replied, adjusting his tassel.

Lucas squinted. "You're thinking about that guy from New York again, huh?"

Matt's jaw tightened. "Yeah. I should've said something. He looked right at me like he knew me."

In the stands, Emma clutched her camera, eyes locked on the stage. Pride burned in her expression, but beneath it was something colder, sharper. She leaned toward Andres and murmured, "I have his memories. I raised him; they didn't. Boo-hoo…get over it. He's mine now."

Andres' jaw flexed. He clapped when Matt's name, "Benjamin Diaz," was called, but each strike of his palms was slow, reluctant, as if weighed down by a truth he could no longer ignore.

"That's my baby!" Emma shouted for the whole auditorium to hear, snapping picture after picture.

Matt stepped onto the stage, diploma in hand. The name echoed in his ears. Diaz... that's not my name. I'm not Ben either.

That night, back in his dorm, he folded clothes into a suitcase. The summer in New York lay ahead not just for medical school, but for answers. The crayon drawing of the Statue of Liberty slid into the side pocket. He wasn't leaving it behind.

Miles away, in a modest New York kitchen, Javier and Elena sat at the table surrounded by notes, phone numbers, and faded flyers.

"I believe he's coming home," Elena whispered.

Javier's fingers tightened on the edge of the table. "I think so too."

His words lingered in the quiet like a prayer not yet answered. And just a state away in Massachusetts, a young man boarded a plane unaware that each mile was carrying him closer to the truth.

Chapter 25
The Return

It had been less than a week since he packed his bag and tucked the crayon drawing inside. Now, stepping off the plane, Matt, 22, felt the hum of New York seep into his bones. Backpack slung over one shoulder, eyes scanning the terminal, he drank in the noise and movement like he'd been starving for it.

The rhythmic screech of subway wheels. The impatient shouts of taxi drivers. The warm aroma of roasted peanuts drifts from a street cart outside. Every sensation felt strangely familiar, as if buried deep in the folds of his memory.

He inhaled slowly. "I'm back."

Lucas clapped him on the shoulder as he stepped off behind him. "Welcome home. Or something like it."

"Yeah," Matt said, his gaze already pulling toward the city. "Something like it."

They grabbed their luggage and headed for a cab. The ride through midtown was a blur of glass towers, honking horns, and hurried footsteps. Every corner was a whisper from another life. As the Statue of Liberty came into view in the distance, Matt pressed his hand against the window.

His chest tightened. I've been there before...

A memory flashed, a smaller hand inside a larger one, the salt bite of the harbor air, a pretzel warm in his palm. His father's laugh. But whose father?

A thousand miles away, the late afternoon sun bore down on Andres Diaz as he leaned on the front gate, chatting with their neighbor, Joe. The talk was easy, weather, yard work, and how the mower blade needed sharpening.

The screen door creaked open behind them.

Emma stepped outside, her smile fixed in that too-bright way that made Andres tense. "Oh, hello there," she said, eyes settling on the small figure who had just wandered out from behind Joe's legs, his six-year-old daughter, Abby, clutching a plastic doll with tangled hair.

Emma's voice softened into a syrupy tone. "Well, aren't you just the prettiest little thing?" she cooed, bending down to Abby's eye level.

Abby gave a shy smile.

"I've always wanted a little girl," Emma said wistfully, eyes flicking briefly toward Andres before settling back on Abby. "Would you like to come inside? I baked cookies this morning... still warm."

Andres's jaw tightened. "Emma. Inside. Now."

She didn't move. "It's just cookies, Andres. I'm being friendly."

Joe's posture stiffened. "Abby, come here, sweetheart."

Abby hesitated, glancing at Emma before darting to her father's side. Joe kept his tone polite but clipped. "We'll... see you around."

They disappeared into their yard. The moment the door shut, Andres turned on Emma.

"What was that?"

Her smile didn't fade. If anything, it sharpened. "You're overreacting. I was making conversation."

"That's not conversation. You can't just take people's children."

Her eyes glinted, the smugness unmistakable. "Why not? I've done it before."

Andres's breath caught. "Do you even hear yourself? We've destroyed lives."

Emma tilted her head, feigning confusion. "Destroyed? No, Andrés. I saved him. Without me, he'd be dead. Instead, he's accomplished, educated, thriving. And if he wants a little sister, why shouldn't he have one?"

"Because she wouldn't be ours," Andres snapped. "No more. This ends here."

She laughed under her breath, a quiet, chilling sound. "You act like I'm the villain. I gave him a future no one else could. I earned him."

Andres stared at her, a cold knot forming in his chest. "You didn't earn him. You stole him. And one day, it's going to catch up to you."

Emma's expression hardened, her voice dropping to a whisper. "Not if I don't let it."

Back in New York, Matt dropped his duffel on the dorm bed that evening, exhaustion heavy in his bones. Outside, the city hummed, alive and unrelenting. He stared out the window at the endless sprawl of lights, the feeling gnawing at him stronger than ever.

Somewhere in this city, his answers waited. And this time, he wasn't leaving without them.

Later that night, Andres sat at the kitchen table, staring into his coffee while Emma flipped through a photo album of Matt's life, her version of it, page after page, smiling school portraits, birthday candles, vacations that never should have been theirs.

"Look at him here," she said, tapping a picture of Matt at twelve. "He's mine. He's always been mine."

Andres's stomach turned. The walls felt smaller, the air heavier. He couldn't get the image of Abby, the little neighbor girl, out of his head.

In that moment, he realized Emma wasn't just holding onto the past. She was hunting for her next chance.

He closed the album with a sharp snap. "This can't happen again," he said, his voice low, final.

Emma smiled faintly, not even looking at him. "We'll see."

Back at the dormitory, Matt sat with Lucas, tapping away on his laptop.

"I found this blog that archives missing children cases from the early 2000s. I cross-referenced everything I remember: statue, fire, green zebra socks, and this came up."

He pointed to a headline: "Four-Year-Old Boy Presumed Dead in New York Fire Still Missing."

Lucas read aloud, "Matthew Colon. Last seen wearing a green and black zebra jacket."

Matt's eyes narrowed. "It... it lines up."

"You don't know for sure," Lucas said carefully.

Matt stared at the screen. "No... but I feel it."

Lucas leaned in. "This is... close. Too close."

Matt stared at the screen. "It matches more than it should. I don't remember everything, but the pieces are fitting together."

Lucas sat back, watching his friend wrestle with the thought. "So, what now?"

Matt closed the laptop slowly, as if sealing a decision inside.

"Now... I follow the trail. Whatever's at the end, I need to see it for myself."

"I need to see where this road leads."

Chapter 26
Time and Tide

Somewhere else, not too far from the dormitory and Matt's quiet resolve, another day was beginning one that carried its memories and unanswered questions.

"Time does not wait for anyone." Elena read the quote on a poster board inside the cozy coffee shop as she pushed open the glass door. The wind caught her scarf gently as she stepped into the morning sun. She took a thoughtful sip from her cup and whispered, "It does not." It had been eighteen years since she last saw her son. He would be twenty-two now. Not a single day passed that she didn't think about him, where he might be, what he might be doing. Was he healthy? Safe? Was he happy? Elena closed her eyes for a moment, feeling the weight of longing settle into her chest.

"Good morning, Elena! How are you today?" said Marcus, one of her coworkers from the front desk." "I'm well, thank you."

"A little birdie told me you're turning forty-four this weekend," he said with a grin. She chuckled. "Yes, I am. My husband is taking me to St. Thomas for a week." "Now that's a birthday celebration if I ever heard one," said Alexis, another colleague, chiming in. "Bring me back a souvenir!"

"Me too!" added Marcus, laughing.

Elena smiled politely and waved them off. Her suitcase was already packed and waiting at home. Every year since Matt went missing, Javier had taken her on exotic trips for her birthday. It was his way of easing her heartache, of helping her step away from the heaviness that hovered over their lives. While it never truly erased the pain, it drew them closer, bound by love and hope.

Back at her desk, Elena moved through her work rhythmically. Her hands were busy, but her mind wandered to sunny beaches and quiet waves.

On the other side of town, Javier was loading packages into his delivery truck, his usual delivery route already mapped in his head. "Hey, Javier!" called the owner of the pizza shop as Javier pulled up to the front. "Thought you'd be on vacation this week."

"Hey, Luigi. We're leaving tonight after work. Got a seven o'clock flight."

"Where are you headed this year?"

"St. Thomas," Javier replied, smiling. "We were in Puerto Rico last week visiting Elena's parents. After St. Thomas, we're hitting Cuba and the Cayman Islands."

"Don't forget last year, you were gone for two weeks! I was begging the transportation company to send someone else for my deliveries," Luigi joked.

They both laughed. Javier waved goodbye. "See you in a week, hombre." As Javier guided the delivery truck through late-afternoon traffic, the hum of the engine was a familiar background to his thoughts. At a red light, his gaze drifted toward a busy pizza parlor on the corner. The door swung open, and two young men stepped out, laughing over something only they understood. One of them was taller, with the same dark hair Javier had seen in a hundred dreams, turned just enough for the sunlight to catch his profile. Javier's breath hitched. His fingers tightened on the steering wheel. "Matthew?" he whispered, the name tumbling out before he could stop it. The light turned green, but his truck idled a heartbeat too long. Cars honked behind him, snapping him out of the trance. By the time he eased forward, the boys were crossing the street, swallowed up in a crowd of pedestrians. He craned his neck, searching for that face again, heart pounding with a mixture of hope and disbelief. Was it really him or just another cruel trick of longing? The traffic carried him onward, but the image stayed, burning into his mind. For the rest of the day, he drove in silence, the world around him a blur, the question echoing over and over: Was that my son?

As the afternoon sun began to dip, Javier returned to the drop-off hub, clocked out, and headed home. He still wasn't able to shake the image from his mind, but he said he wasn't going to tell Elena. As he entered his home, he met with Elena, who was upstairs, adding last-minute essentials to her bag.

He kissed her on the cheek and leaned against the bedroom doorway. "Hey, honey, ready to go?"

"Almost! I just thought of a few more things at work," she replied, beaming.

Within an hour, a taxi driver pulled into their driveway. Javier wheeled their luggage to the trunk while Elena slipped into the backseat.

"I wanted to say thank you," Elena said softly as they pulled away from their house. "For always taking me away every year... for giving me something to look forward to."

He turned toward her, taking her hand in his. "We've been through a lot, Elena. You have carried more than anyone should. These trips... they are for both of us. I love you."

She leaned over and kissed him on the lips. "And I love you."

The airport was bustling when they arrived. Lines snaked through terminals, luggage carts squeaked across polished floors, and flight announcements echoed overhead. But none of it mattered. For Elena, each step closer to their gate felt like an exhale.

Once seated at the gate, Javier pulled out a small, neatly folded photo. It was worn and faded, a crayon drawing of a boy at the Statue of Liberty, scrawled by a child's hand. Elena caught sight of it and froze.

"That drawing..."

"I keep it in my wallet," Javier said. "It reminds me of the day he made it. He was so excited about that trip."

She nodded slowly. "I remember. We bought him that little foam crown. He wouldn't take it off."

There was silence between them, but it wasn't hollow. It was thick with memory and emotion.

"Do you still think about that boy from the hotel?" she asked.

"Every day. I should've said something. I should've followed him more closely."

"You did what you could. It's not your fault. If he's alive... if that was him... We'll find him."

Their flight began boarding. Javier placed the drawing back into his wallet and took Elena's hand.

Not too far away, Matt stood in his dorm on campus. His degree, framed and resting on the desk, was from a prestigious university.

He finally unpacked the remaining boxes and organized everything neatly. His mind, however, was in disarray from the daily searches he conducted with Lucas. He held the same drawing, a crayon picture of the Statue of Liberty, that he had kept folded in a book since childhood. The details were fading, but the emotion remained fresh.

"That trip... I was there. But not with Emma and Andres. Someone else took me. I know it." His memory was still fractured, but this much was clear: New York wasn't just a city. It was the key. He placed the drawing inside his journal and put it back in the drawer. "I'm here for answers," he whispered. "And maybe... just maybe, for family."

Back in St. Thomas, Elena and Javier walked along the beach, hand in hand, letting the warm tide wash over their feet. Palm trees danced in the breeze, and waves whispered along the shore. "Do you believe in fate?" Elena asked suddenly. "Sometimes. Why?" "Today, when I was walking out of the coffee shop, there was a poster that said, 'Time does not wait for anyone.' And I thought it's time. Maybe he's already out there looking for us."

Javier squeezed her hand. "Then we'll be here. Waiting. Hoping." They watched the sunset in silence, the horizon glowing like a promise yet to be fulfilled.

Chapter 27
Anchored in Hope

The morning light poured through the wide balcony doors, filling the suite with the soft shimmer of ocean waves. Elena stood barefoot on the balcony, coffee cup in hand, breathing in the salt-kissed air. Below, the beach was already alive with early risers strolling along the shore, their laughter drifting upward.

Javier emerged from the bedroom, adjusting his watch. "You've been out here a while," he said, slipping an arm around her waist.

"I didn't want to miss this view," she replied, leaning into him. "It feels like the world finally slowed down."

On the coffee table inside lay a stack of glossy brochures they'd picked up the night before in the hotel lobby. One in particular had caught Elena's eye, a catamaran sailing along the St. Thomas coast. She picked it up again now.

"I still want to do this," she said, tapping the cover.

"Whatever you want, honey," Javier said with a smile. "First, let's get some breakfast."

They dined at the gourmet restaurant, the hotel's airy breakfast cafe. The scent of warm pastries, fresh fruit, and roasted coffee filled the space.

"So, you want to try catamaran sailing?" Javier asked between bites of his croissant. "Yes"

Elena opened the brochure again. "Or we can try stand-up paddleboarding."

Javier laughed. "That's exactly what I was about to suggest. Want to give it a try?"

She raised an eyebrow. "Stand-up paddleboarding? You mean balancing on a floating board while paddling across the ocean?"

He grinned. "Exactly that.

She shook her head, chuckling. "Let's do it. But if I fall in, you're taking me to dinner tonight."

Back in their room, Javier changed into black swim trunks while Elena emerged from the bathroom in a sleek, black high-neck bikini. Javier paused when he saw her.

"Do we even need to leave this room?" he asked playfully, his eyes never leaving hers.

Elena smirked and walked over to him. He pulled her close, gently brushing his lips against her neck. "I love you so much," he whispered.

They shared a slow, passionate moment, letting the warmth of love and desire ground them in each other's arms. It was a rare kind of stillness, the kind they needed.

Later, they headed to the water sports station, life jackets strapped on, boards balanced in the surf.

"Okay, let's see if we can do this without looking ridiculous," Elena said, laughing nervously.

They paddled around, slowly gaining confidence. Locals waved from the shore, and a group of kids cheered them on.

"You're doing great," Javier said. "Look at you balancing like a pro."

Elena giggled. "I'm trying not to die out here, Javier."

They paddled back to the beach, exhilarated and slightly exhausted. As they lay on their towels under a thatched umbrella, Elena turned to him.

"It feels like we can breathe again here. I don't know how to explain it."

He nodded. "It's the ocean. It listens. It heals. It speaks without words."

As the sun began its descent, casting gold across the waves, they walked hand in hand along the beach. Seagulls floated overhead, and the world seemed to pause.

"Javier," Elena said softly, "do you think he still thinks about us?"

Javier paused, heart heavy. "I don't know. But I hope so. I hope he knows we never stopped looking. That we never gave up."

She stopped walking, turning to face the horizon. "I dream of him often. Not the child we lost, but the man he's become. I don't know what he looks like anymore, but I feel him. In here." She placed her hand on her heart.

"Then he's not lost," Javier said, pulling her close. "He's just... not yet found."

Elena whispered a quiet prayer into the wind. "Wherever you are, Matt... may God cover you. May you know love, and may we find our way back to you."

Javier added, his voice thick with emotion, "And may we have the strength to wait, to believe, and to hope."

The waves rolled on. The stars began to appear. And in the quiet peace of that St. Thomas evening, two hearts held fast to faith, anchored in love, and tethered to a reunion they still believed would one day come. They stood in silence as the tide kissed their toes, wrapped in the embrace of hope and the eternal rhythm of the sea.

While they held onto peace in St. Thomas, far away in New York, a storm was quietly gathering.

Chapter 28
The Measure of Our Days

A few days after Javier and Elena arrived in St. Thomas, life back home continued with a quieter rhythm, though not without its trials. In New York, at the Colon family home, Vera was in the kitchen preparing tea when a violent cough overtook her. She stumbled to the bathroom, the taste of iron rising in her throat. As she leaned over the sink, blood splattered the basin.

She wiped her mouth with trembling hands, staining the tissue deep red. Another wave of nausea struck. George, who had been reading in the living room, came rushing to the door.

"Vera? What's going on? Are you okay?" he asked, voice laced with panic.

She turned to him slowly, her lips pale. "I think I need to see Dr. Thomas."

George wasted no time. He helped her into their large white SUV, his hands shaking as he buckled her seatbelt. As they drove, Vera grew weaker, and before they reached the main road, George had to pull over. She opened the door and vomited again, twice as much blood this time. Her skin was ghostly white, and her eyes glossed over.

"Hold on, baby. Just hold on," he whispered, pressing the gas pedal harder.

At the hospital emergency entrance, George carried Vera in his arms, his cries echoing through the sterile hallway. "Somebody help us!"

A team of nurses and doctors rushed out, taking Vera from his arms and rolling her into the back for urgent care.

George collapsed into a chair in the waiting area, staring at his bloodied hands. He wanted to call Javier, but he knew his son was still in St. Thomas. Vera had insisted that he not be disturbed unless necessary.

Hours passed like days. Finally, a young doctor in a navy-blue coat stepped out. "Is there a George Colon here?"

George bolted upright. "Yes, I'm George. Is my wife okay?"

"Please, come with me."

He followed in silence. The antiseptic scent grew stronger the farther they walked. They turned into a quiet recovery room where Vera lay propped up in bed, a thin IV tube snaking from her arm.

"You're awake," George said as he hurried to her bedside, tears forming in his eyes.

"Yes. I'm okay for now," she whispered.

"What's going on, Vera? Tell me."

She didn't sugarcoat it. "The cancer is back. After eight years in remission, it's returned... stage four."

George covered his mouth and let out a broken sob. "No. No, Vera. We just celebrated our fiftieth anniversary. You can't go. I wouldn't know what to do without you."

She touched his face gently. "I'm not gone yet. But my body's tired. Still, I have one thing left to do. I need to see Chico. I can't leave this earth without seeing our grandson again."

George wanted to believe that was possible. Maybe hope alone could keep her alive a little longer.

"Did you call Javier?" she asked.

"No. I was waiting to speak with you first. He should be flying back tomorrow."

"Leave him a message, but don't tell him why. Let him enjoy the flight back in peace."

George nodded, though every part of him wanted to scream for his son to come immediately.

Later, as night fell over the city, George sat beside Vera's hospital bed, his hand wrapped around hers.

He prayed aloud, voice breaking: "Lord, you brought us together fifty years ago. You've blessed our family, our home, and our love. I ask now in Jesus' name, please heal my Vera. She is the heart of this family. We've obeyed Your word and kept Your commandments. Please, Lord... give us more time."

Vera opened her eyes, calm and steady. "Honey, remember Psalm 39:4 KJV: 'Lord, make me to know mine end, and the measure of my days, what it is; that I may know how frail I am.'"

She took a deep breath. "I have peace, George. We're only here for a little while. But while we are, we must live with purpose and trust in God's timing."

George nodded, resting his forehead gently against hers.

Just then, a nurse quietly entered the room, bringing in warm broth and ginger tea. "This should help settle her stomach," she said kindly.

Vera smiled and thanked her, sipping slowly while George stroked her hair.

"Do you think we'll see him again?" George asked after a long silence.

Vera looked out the window, where the moonlight illuminated the skyline. "I know we will maybe not tomorrow, or even this year. But God didn't give me this burden without a reason. That boy is out there, George. I feel it in my soul. And he's searching for us, too."

Her voice held conviction, and it calmed George's spirit just enough to smile.

"I'll leave the message for Javier tonight. I'll ask him to come straight to the hospital in the morning," he said.

As George stepped out into the hallway to make the call, Vera whispered one last prayer into the night:

"Lord, I trust You. I may be frail in body, but my hope is anchored in You. If it is your will, let me see my grandson before I go. But even if not, I will praise You still."

Outside the hospital, the wind picked up slightly, sweeping through the parking lot like a gentle echo of her faith. And in that quiet room, Vera lay resting, held not only by IV tubes and medications, but by belief, unshaken.

The next morning, when Javier and Elena stepped off the plane in New York, his phone buzzed. A single voicemail notification glowed on the screen: his father. He pressed play and lifted it to his ear.

"Javier, come to the hospital."

The words were few, but they carried a weight that pressed into his chest. He turned to Elena. "It's my dad. We need to go now."

She nodded, her face pale. "Lord, I pray everything is okay."

"Me too," Javier murmured as they hurried toward the exit.

Chapter 29
The Prayer Answered

The sunlight of St. Thomas still clung to their skin, but the warmth was already fading. In its place came a cold urgency neither could explain. They slid into the back of a taxi, Javier giving the driver the hospital's address without hesitation.

Outside, the city moved at its usual relentless pace. Inside the car, silence reigned, the kind that comes when prayers are whispered but answers haven't arrived yet. He listened to a second voicemail. "Javier... It's your mom. She's in the hospital. Room 163, first floor. Come quick."

Forty-five minutes later, their cab screeched to a stop outside the hospital. They didn't bother with their luggage, just hauled it along behind them, wheels clattering across the tile as they rushed to the front desk.

"We're here to see Vera Colon," Javier said, breathless.

"Room 163. First floor. Down the hall to your right," the receptionist replied.

They didn't wait for further directions. Javier pushed forward, his pace quickening with each step until they reached the door. His hand hovered on the handle for a heartbeat before he eased it open.

And there she was.

Vera lay propped up in bed, thinner than when they last saw her, her once-strong hands resting against a pale hospital blanket. Yet her eyes were still bright, still filled with the kind of faith that could split the sea, locked on her son the moment he entered.

George sat beside her, his fingers curled around a Styrofoam coffee cup as if it were the only thing keeping him steady.

"Hey, baby," Vera said, her voice gentle, a smile curling the corners of her lips. "Come here."

Javier dropped his bags and was at her side in two strides, pulling her fragile frame into his arms. He kissed her forehead, holding her like the boy who used to run to her after scraped knees and long days. Elena stepped in quietly, setting the luggage aside and reaching for Vera's hand.

George's voice was low but firm. "Sit down, son."

Javier sat, his hands trembling. He hadn't been ready for this. Not this soon.

Vera didn't waste words. "Javier... I didn't want to tell you before. Not while you were searching for Matt. But I'm sick again."

Javier's stomach dropped. "Sick? What do you mean...?"

"The cancer is back. Stage four." Her eyes softened as his filled with tears. "But I'm not gone yet. And I've been asking God for one more thing before He calls me home."

She took his hand, squeezing weakly. "I need to see Chico before I go."

The air in the room thickened with silence. Javier bowed his head, unable to speak. Elena gripped Vera's other hand, tears streaming freely.

A knock broke the stillness.

The door opened, and a tall man in a white coat stepped in, followed by a small group of residents. "Mrs. Colon, I'm Dr. Thomas. I'm here with some of our brightest first-year doctors."

One by one, they introduced themselves.

"Dr. Gabriel Sanchez."

"Dr. Mia Davis."

"Dr. Sofia Lewinsky."

Then the last resident stepped forward. "Hi, I'm Dr. Mat..."

Vera's breath caught. She sat upright, her eyes wide. "Chico." Her voice was clear, firm, and unwavering. "That's Chico. I'd know my grandson's smile anywhere. You have your mother's eyes."

The room froze.

Matt blinked. "What... did you just call me?"

Vera's hands trembled, but she certainly did not. "Javier, it's Chico. Elena, it's Matt."

Matt stared, confused. "How do you know my name is Matt?"

Dr. Thomas glanced around, sensing the gravity of the moment. "Let's give the family some privacy." He ushered the other residents out.

When the door closed, Javier rose to his feet, his voice breaking. "You're our son. Matthew Colon. We lost you when you were four years old."

Elena clutched her chest, sobbing. "We've prayed for this day," she whispered.

Matt shook his head slowly. "I was told my name was Matthew "Ben" Diaz. But I always knew… Diaz wasn't right. I could never remember my last name, but I knew it started with a C."

He turned to Javier, eyes narrowing with recognition. "Wait… I saw you once. Five years ago. A hotel lobby. You were making a delivery. You looked at me like… like you knew me."

Javier's tears fell freely now. "I did. I didn't have a way to find you."

Javier stepped forward and embraced him fully, fiercely. "You weren't imagining it. I knew, son. God, I knew."

They held each other, both shaking with sobs.

Elena approached slowly, her hands trembling. Matt turned to her, his voice breaking. "I'm sorry I left the police station."

"I'm sorry, I left you alone in the apartment that night."

She pulled him into her arms. "No, baby. I'm sorry. I should have never left you alone."

Javier looked toward the bed. "Matt… these are your grandparents. George and Vera Colon."

Matt hugged George, who clung to him with the strength of decades of loss and longing. Then Matt turned to Vera's bedside.

Her smile was pure peace. "I knew it was you," she whispered. "You have your mother's eyes… and her heart."

Matt knelt beside her, taking her frail hand in his. "I'm here, Grandma."

"Chico…" her voice was as thin as the hospital sheets, "you grew up so fast. I missed so much."

His throat closed. "You were always with me. Somehow… I always felt you there."

Her lips curved faintly. "You made me proud… You grew up to be something special."

And then, almost singing, she spoke,

"I love you… You don't know how much I love you…"

Her eyes fluttered closed, her hand still in his.

The room was silent except for the sound of hearts breaking and prayers being whispered all at once. The hours after their reunion passed in a blur of tears, laughter, and long-overdue words. Even after Matt left the hospital that night, the sound of his grandmother's voice lingered in his mind, her blessing wrapping around him like a warm quilt. Javier and Elena had asked him to visit their home when he felt ready. For two days, Matt wrestled with the weight of the past and the pull of something new until at last, he knew it was time.

Chapter 30
A Home Once Lost

Two days after the emotional reunion at the hospital, Matt agreed to meet Javier and Elena at their home. Though his heart pounded with anxiety, he couldn't ignore the pull in his chest…something told him this meeting would bring clarity, peace, and perhaps, healing.

As the taxi driver pulled into the quiet neighborhood where the Colon home stood, Matt's palms grew damp. The house was a modest two-story brick home with a white porch swing swaying in the gentle breeze. Javier stepped out onto the porch before Matt even knocked, as if he had been watching and waiting for his arrival.

"Hey, son," Javier said, his voice warm but trembling with emotion.

Matt nodded, his throat too tight to speak. Elena appeared in the doorway, eyes already glistening.

"Come in," she said softly.

Matt stepped inside and was immediately enveloped by a sense of belonging. The house smelled of warm, familiar cinnamon and coffee. He looked around, taking in the photos on the wall. A framed picture near the entrance caught his attention: a chubby-cheeked baby wrapped in a blue blanket.

"Is that…" he began, pointing.

Elena nodded. "That's you. Javier took that photo at the hospital, just minutes after you were born."

Matt stepped closer, studying the infant's face. "I don't think I've ever seen a baby picture of myself," he murmured. "Andres and Emma… they never showed me one. I always thought that was strange."

Elena crossed to a nearby cabinet and opened it. "After the fire, we lost everything we owned," she said softly. "But your grandparents, George and Vera, had kept some of your belongings at their house, and thank God for that. Your grandmother loved taking pictures of you, and she saved them."

She pulled out an old leather-bound album, its corners worn smooth with age, and slowly opened it. Inside was a flood of images: Matt's first smile, his baptism, his tiny feet cradled in Javier's hand. "This is how we kept your memory alive."

Tears welled in Matt's eyes. "This is me," he whispered. "It's like rediscovering a piece of myself I didn't know was missing."

Javier, now seated across from him, pulled out another photo from a separate envelope. It was Matt's fourth birthday party. He was grinning from ear to ear, seated in a bright red Truck with big wheels, an electric car. Behind him stood Javier, wearing a party hat and holding a balloon.

"That Truck was your favorite," Javier chuckled, the memory tugging at his heart.

"I… I think I remember that car," Matt said, a look of realization washing over him. "It's like a flash. A moment. But it felt like a dream."

Javier leaned forward, his eyes locking with Matt's. "You are our son, Matthew Colon. We lost you, but we never gave up hope. I know your memories were taken or buried, but the truth never left us."

Matt's eyes were brimming with emotion. He stared down at the photographs, each one a truth carved in time. "For years, I've asked myself who I am. And now… now I finally know."

He stood and walked around the living room, absorbing every picture, every artifact of the childhood he never knew he had. Drawings from preschool. A lock of baby hair. A preschool fingerprint painting.

"I lived a lie," he said softly. "Andres and Emma raised me, yes, but they never gave me this. They never told me who I was."

Elena approached him, placing her hand on his shoulder. "You didn't live a lie, Matthew. Your grandmother took many photos of you, which helped preserve your memories despite the fire that occurred that night. You lived in survival. That is different. And now, you get to live in truth."

Matt turned to her and embraced her tightly. "I missed all of this. I missed you."

She wept into his shoulder. "And we missed you every single day. Every birthday. Every holiday. Every moment that passed without you."

Javier wrapped his arms around both of them. "We don't want to waste any more time. We want you in our lives, Matt. However much you're willing to give."

"I want that too," Matt replied. "I don't know what it will look like, or how we heal all this, but I want to start."

They sat down on the couch together and began flipping through more albums. Elena brought out a small wooden box from the hallway closet. Inside were baby clothes, tiny onesies, hospital bracelets, and a soft blue beanie with "Matthew" embroidered across the front.

Matt picked it up delicately, as if it might vanish. "This is mine?"

"Yes," Elena smiled through her tears. "I knitted it for you the day before you were born."

Javier pulled out a video cassette tape. "And this," he said, "is your first birthday party. We've digitized it, but I kept the original."

They laughed, cried, and talked late into the night. Matt learned stories of his infancy, his first word, "Agua", his obsession with building blocks, and his favorite lullaby that Elena used to hum.

With every detail, his identity stitched itself back together.

Later that evening, as he stood in the doorway ready to leave, Matt turned around.

"Can I stay overnight?" he said. I want to know everything. About whom I was. About whom we were."

Javier stepped forward, his voice steady but thick with emotion. "This house, this family, will always be open to you. You were never forgotten, Matt. You were always our son."

Matt gave them both a hug. "Thank you for not giving up on me."

Elena whispered, "Never."

Chapter 31
A Grandmother's Goodbye

Matthew stayed the night at his parents' house.

Sleep came slowly… but it came peacefully.

For the first time in years, he wasn't waking up in a world that felt borrowed.

This felt like home.

When he opened his eyes the next morning, the smell of breakfast drifted into the room: eggs, bacon, and pancakes. The aroma wrapped around him like a warm embrace.

He followed it to the kitchen, where Elena was plating food. Javier sat at the table, sipping coffee.

"Good morning, sweetheart," Elena smiled, the smile only a mother can give.

"Morning," Matt replied. "Something smells amazing."

"Eat up," Javier said, motioning to the seat beside him. "Your favorites… even if you didn't know they were your favorites yet."

They laughed one of those healing laughs that comes when walls start to come down.

But as they ate, Matt's tone shifted.

"I know who took me from the police station eighteen years ago," he said quietly. "Andres and Emma Diaz. They need to be arrested."

Elena's fork froze in midair.

Javier leaned forward. "Are you sure?"

"Yes. I remember now. Pieces came back after I saw the name Colon... but when I saw that baby picture of me, it all clicked. They stole me. And they lied for almost two decades."

Elena reached for his hand. "We want justice too. But first, we want you safe."

Matt nodded. "I'm going to file a report. They need to be held accountable."

Before more could be said, Javier's phone buzzed on the counter. He glanced at the screen.

"Hey, Dad... What's going on?"

Matt watched as Javier's expression changed.

"Okay. We'll be right there."

He turned to Elena and Matt.

"It's Mom. We need to get to the hospital."

Twenty minutes later, they walked into the waiting room.

George was there, head in his hands. When he saw them, he stood.

"She took a turn this morning. She's asking for you, Matt."

Matt's chest tightened. He walked down the corridor, his legs heavy.

Inside the room, Vera lay in bed, frail but awake.

"Chico," she whispered.

Matt went to her side and took her hand. "I'm here, Grandma."

Her smile was soft but steady. "God answered my prayer. I saw you before I left this world."

Tears blurred his vision. "You gave me hope before I even knew who I was. You held on for me. Thank you."

Her fingers squeezed his lightly.

"You are our legacy, Matthew. You carry our faith, our strength. Promise me you'll walk in truth… and never let go of God."

"I promise."

She glanced at Javier and Elena, then back to Matt.

"Take care of them. They suffered more than anyone should."

A soft breath left her lungs. Her hand went limp.

"Grandma?" Matt whispered.

The monitor flatlined.

Elena cried out. Javier pulled her close.

George stood silently in the doorway, his eyes wet.

A nurse entered quietly to confirm the time.

The funeral was held four days later, at the church Vera had loved all her life.

Her favorite hymns filled the sanctuary.

The altar was covered in lilies, her favorite flower.

Matt stepped to the pulpit, paper trembling in his hands.

"I didn't get twenty years with my grandmother like I should have… but I got a moment that changed my life.

"I met a woman whose love waited for me longer than most people could bear. Vera Colon was more than a grandmother. She was the backbone of a family that refused to give up.

"She taught me something in the last few days that I'll carry forever—faith is not about what we see… It's about what we believe is possible.

"She waited for me. She believed. And that belief… saved me.

"I love you, Grandma. Thank you for never giving up hope. I promise to live a life worthy of the love you gave me."

The sanctuary was silent, except for muffled sobs.

Matt stepped down, joining his family in the front pew.

Javier's arm went around his shoulder. Elena leaned her head on him.

In grief, there was peace.

Vera's prayer had been answered.

Her spirit now lived on in the son and grandson she had waited a lifetime to hold.

And though their hearts were heavy, the legacy of faith… carried them forward. The echoes of Vera's hymns still lingered in Matt's mind as night fell. Sleep didn't come easily; his dreams were filled with flashes of her smile, her voice urging him to keep his promise. By the time dawn broke, the weight of goodbye still pressed against his chest. As morning light spilled across the familiar walls, the joy of being together again carried a quiet truth:

finding each other was only the beginning; now they had to learn how to be a family again."

Chapter 32
Grace

The morning after the funeral, the house was quiet. Grief hung in the air like a thick mist, heavy and unforgiving. Matt had stayed the night with his parents, needing the comfort of their presence and the grounding of their home.

He woke to the scent of fresh coffee and sizzling bacon. In the kitchen, Elena offered a small, gentle smile as she set a plate in front of him. Javier poured coffee and slid the mug his way.

"Thanks," Matt murmured, taking a seat.

For a while, they ate in silence, the only sounds the clink of silverware and the hum of the refrigerator. Then Matt set his fork down. "I need to tell you something."

Javier and Elena looked up.

"They need to be arrested," Matt said flatly.

Elena's fork paused midair. "Matt…"

"No," he cut in. "I know they raised me. I know they fed me, clothed me. But they stole me. They lied to me every single day. And now… now Grandma's gone. I'll never get those years back."

Javier reached across the table, his hand warm over Matt's. "Son, we understand. And we'll stand with you."

Matt's voice shook. "They robbed me of my life. They robbed all of us."

"We'll go with you," Elena said, steady and sure. "To the police station. We'll tell them everything."

Matt nodded, swallowing hard. The warmth of the kitchen, once a place of laughter and family rituals, felt colder now, edged with the finality of truth, no more hiding. No more trying to make peace with a past that was never his.

The morning wore on slowly. Javier made a few phone calls to community activists and church leaders, while Matt sat quietly on the back porch, staring at the garden his grandmother had once tended. Her lavender bushes still bloomed, faint purple tufts swaying in the early breeze. A single monarch butterfly landed on one of the blossoms, and for a moment, Matt allowed himself to believe it was hope. Watching. Listening. Understanding.

When it was time to leave, Matt changed into a clean shirt and jeans. Elena handed him a small notebook.

"What's this?" he asked.

"Your notes. From when the memories started coming back. I typed them up last night. I thought you might want to bring them with you to the police."

Matt stared at the cover. Ben's Journal. That was the name he had written at the top when he first started questioning everything. He gave a small, tired smile. "Thank you."

The drive to the police station was quiet. Each street corner they passed seemed familiar now, even though Matt did not spend most of his childhood in this town. It was like the veil had been lifted. The city that once felt like home now held a dozen lies at every turn.

As they pulled into the parking lot of the local police station. Matt's stomach tightened. He sat still for a moment, staring at the building's glass doors. He had walked through those same doors as a toddler, lost, confused, and waiting to be claimed. And now, he returned as a grown man, ready to reclaim the truth.

"Are you sure you want to do this today?" Elena asked gently.

Matt opened the door. "I have to."

Inside, the lobby was sterile and still. The receptionist looked up from her computer, offering a polite nod.

"Can I help you?"

Matt hesitated. "I'd like to speak with a detective. It's about a cold case. A kidnapping. From eighteen years ago."

The woman blinked. "Do you have a name or case number?"

Matt turned to Javier, who had already pulled a file from his coat pocket. "The missing person report was filed by Elena and Javier Colon in 1995. The child's name was Matthew Colon."

The woman's eyes widened. "One moment, please."

They were led to a waiting room. The clock ticked slowly. Matt shifted in his seat, scanning the room, the worn carpet, the chipped paint, the buzzing fluorescent lights. It was surreal. This was where it all started. And, hopefully, where it would end.

After twenty minutes, a detective entered mid-fifties, gray at the temples, calm but cautious.

"I'm Detective Rosalind Kramer," she said, extending her hand. "You said this is about the Colon kidnapping?"

"Yes," Matt said, rising to shake her hand. "I'm the kid who went missing."

Kramer blinked, her mouth slightly open. "Come again?"

"My name is Matthew Colon. I was taken from the police station the day after the fire. I was raised under the name Benjamin Diaz. But that's not who I am. I have proof."

He handed over the folder, along with the notebook Elena had given him.

Detective Kramer flipped through the documents, her expression tightening. "We'll need to run this through Missing Persons and reopen the file. If what you're saying is true… this is going to trigger a full investigation."

Matt nodded. "That's what I want."

Kramer looked up. "Do you know who took you?"

"Yes. Andres and Emma Diaz. They're the ones who raised me. Emma claimed I was her son, Ben… but I wasn't. Her real son died. She replaced him with me."

The room fell silent.

Kramer took a deep breath. "Do you know where they are now?"

"They moved to Florida. Their address is in Jacksonville. I'm sure your department can track them." I went to the precinct about five years ago to explain my situation, but no one believed me."

Kramer scribbled notes. "We'll start there. Thank you for coming forward, Matthew. I know this couldn't have been easy, and I'm truly sorry that this matter was not addressed five years ago, but we will look into it."

"It's not about being easy," Matt said quietly. "It's about what's right."

Before leaving the police station, Javier went to the church to meet with community leaders regarding Matthew's case. They also held a brief news broadcast about their missing son. They wanted justice.

Later that evening, Matt returned home feeling exhausted but lighter, as a weight had finally been lifted. He sat on the living room couch with Elena and Javier, watching an old family video play in the background. He barely recognized the little boy in the tape, but he recognized the smile. The laughter. The love.

"I kept thinking... if I did this, if I told the police, I'd feel angry," Matt said, his voice barely above a whisper. "But I don't. I feel... sad."

Elena wrapped her arms around him. "That's okay, baby. Grief and justice often walk side by side."

He nodded into her shoulder.

A knock on the door interrupted the moment. Javier rose to answer it. Standing outside was a woman in her mid-thirties, with short, curly hair and nervous hands clutching a manila envelope.

"Can I help you?" Javier asked.

"I... I .. I'm Emma's niece," the woman said.

Matt stood slowly. "What?"

She looked at him, tears forming. "My name is Grace. Grace Morales. Emma Diaz is my aunt. I grew up hearing whispers about what happened... and when I heard about your story, word traveled fast on the streets, I knew."

Elena's eyes widened.

Grace nodded. "It's already circulating. 'Missing Boy Found After Eighteen Years.' I just... I wanted to meet you. And I thought you should have this."

She handed Matt the envelope. Inside were several photographs and a letter.

"I found it in my mother's attic after Jacob's death. She was never the same after he died. She didn't talk about it... But she saved these. I thought you might need to see."

Matt's hands shook as he pulled out the photos. One showed Carlos and Ben as toddlers, confused, holding a stuffed bear. Another was a grainy photo of a hospital ID bracelet with the name "Ben D."

And the letter... it was addressed to "The boy I couldn't let go."

Matt's eyes hadn't left Grace since she stepped into the living room, her presence like a ghost from a life he hadn't chosen. The envelope in his lap felt heavier than any truth he'd carried before. Javier and Elena sat in silent tension, their faces unreadable.

Grace took a long breath, then began.

"I don't know how much you already know, so I'll just start from where it all began when everything in our family broke."

Her hands trembled in her lap. "Emma wasn't always unstable. She was anxious, sure, and overprotective. But after Jacob died, something inside her snapped."

Matt oversaw her. "How did Jacob die?"

Grace's throat tightened. "Jacob died of SIDS. Then she later had Carlos and Ben. Emma was bathing Ben. He was four years old. Carlos, my cousin, her older son, was playing upstairs. He climbed up on the banister and fell to the ground. Emma panicked. She ran to him, screaming, thinking he was dead. She left Ben in the tub."

Elena's breath caught. Grace's eyes welled.

"By the time she came back... Ben had drowned. She just... forgot he was in there."

Matt's chest rose and fell with restrained grief. "And Carlos?"

Grace looked down. "I was told he died, too. I heard he was taken away in the ambulance and didn't make it. That's what Andres told the family. But Emma never believed Ben was gone. She started saying things, things that didn't make sense."

"What kind of things?" Javier asked gently.

"She said God had taken Ben but promised to return him in another form. That He would give her a second chance if she were ready to receive him."

Matt's jaw tensed.

"She started watching kids in parks. Grocery stores. Malls. She would stare at little boys and whisper to herself. Said she was looking for signs of marks, voices, a familiar smile."

Grace shook her head. "Then one day, she brought home a young child. Said it was Ben. No one believed her. He had a completely different hair texture and eye color from hers. But Andres backed her up. He always did."

Matt leaned forward. "What was his name?"

"Elijah Gonzalez. He was four years old when she took him. She kidnapped him from a mall in New Jersey. His mom had turned around for a minute. Emma just... vanished with him."

Elena's eyes went wide with horror.

"They moved. Emma convinced herself that Elijah was Ben. She dressed him in Ben's old clothes, wrapped him in Ben's blanket, and sang him the same lullabies. Every time he called her 'Mommy,' it just made the lie feel more real."

Matt's voice dropped. "What happened to him?"

Grace's expression collapsed. I don't know, but I think something bad happened to him.

Matt's breath caught.

The room was silent.

"And that's when everything unraveled," Grace continued. "Emma had a complete psychotic break."

Matt stared at her.

"You were at the police station found during the chaos after the apartment's fire. You were with a police officer. Quiet. Confused. She walked in and told the officers that you were her son. That your name was Ben Diaz, she even cried on cue. Said you'd been lost in the fire."

"Did they believe her?" Elena asked, horrified.

"She presented Ben Diaz's birth certificate to the officer on duty. You didn't remember anything clearly; trauma does that. So, when she hugged you and whispered 'Hi, Ben,' you didn't pull away."

Matt sat back, stunned. "I thought... maybe she was familiar."

"You probably wanted to believe it," Grace said softly. "It's easier than believing you were taken."

Matt looked down at the photos spilling from the envelope... images of him as a child, with forced smiles, staged birthdays, eyes that never truly looked alive.

Grace continued. "I stayed away after that. I couldn't bear to watch. But two years ago, I found the letter. It was in my mother's attic—tucked inside a Holy Scripture. A letter to 'the son I chose.' She said God gave her another chance. He took her sons so she could become a better mother to someone else. She called you her redemption."

Matt's face darkened.

Grace reached across the table, hesitant. "I didn't come for forgiveness. I came because… It's time the truth came out."

Matt nodded, his voice barely a whisper. "Come with me."

"Where?"

"To the police station. Detective Kramer is reopening my case. They need to hear your story, in your words. You saw everything. You lived it. You can confirm what they did to me, what they did to their children."

Grace hesitated, then nodded. "Let's go."

They returned to the police station just before sunset. The clouds had thickened, as if even the sky anticipated a reckoning. Detective Kramer met them in a private room.

"This is Grace Harper," Matt said. "Emma Diaz's niece. She has information about my case and others. She's ready to talk."

Kramer nodded. "We're recording. Please start at the beginning."

Grace told it all: Ben's death, Carlos' fall, the lie about his death, a kidnapping from Jersey, and Emma's psychotic delusions that led her to steal Matthew. Her voice cracked, but she didn't stop. She spoke with the urgency of a woman releasing twenty years of pain and family secrets, and Matt sat beside her, silent but strong.

Kramer's pen scratched furiously across the yellow legal pad, her hand never stopping, her gaze fixed on Matt as he recounted the details. The room was windowless, the kind of place that seemed to swallow time. A faint hum from the overhead fluorescent light filled the silence between questions.

With each word Matt spoke, Kramer's expression shifted, caution giving way to unease, unease hardening into something sharper. Determination. She leaned back, exhaling through her nose as if making a decision she'd been holding off for too long.

"I'm forwarding this to the federal task force on interstate child abductions," she said at last, rising from her chair. "They've been monitoring the Diaz couple in Florida for years, but without hard evidence, it's been a dead end. With your statement and these connections, we'll have enough to push for a warrant by morning."

Her tone wasn't dramatic, but it carried the weight of movement, the kind that could end decades of unanswered questions.

As she stepped out into the hall to make the call, the door eased open again. Another figure entered, moving with the quiet confidence of someone who didn't waste steps.

He was tall, his build lean but solid, eyes sharp enough to make Matt glance away. His badge was clipped to his vest, catching a glint from the overhead light. He paused just inside the doorway, scanning the room like a man who had been here before in another lifetime.

"Officer Dawson," Kramer said from the hall, her voice carrying back through the open door. "He'll be assisting with the reopening of the case."

The man gave Matt a long, unreadable look, no introduction beyond the name. No handshake. Just a single, deliberate nod toward Grace, who sat beside Matt.

"Glad to help," he said.

He took the chair in the corner, notepad closed, pen untouched. He sat like someone who knew how to listen, not just hear. His gaze stayed fixed on a spot on the wall, as if distance helped him focus.

When he finally spoke, his tone was calm but confident.

"We'll find them," he said, not looking at Matt or Grace.

"And when we do, they'll answer for everything."

Chapter 33
Reckoning in the Sun

The Florida heat was already thick and restless by 6:00 a.m., clinging to the air like a warning. The modest home on a quiet street in Jacksonville stood still, front porch cluttered with faded flowerpots, blinds drawn, and no signs of the storm on the horizon.

Inside, Emma Diaz was wide awake.

She stood at the kitchen sink, gently humming as she folded a small yellow blanket that had been washed so many times its edges had thinned to threads. Her lips moved in silent prayer, her eyes glazed but hopeful.

"Today," she whispered to the silence. "He'll come back. My Ben always finds me."

In the living room, Andres sat hunched forward on the couch, the TV remote in hand, but the screen was black. He hadn't slept all night. He had stopped trying long ago. The news out of New York was making its way through underground channels. He'd heard enough to feel the walls closing in.

He looked at Emma now, humming her lullaby with a ghost-like smile. There were no more lies to keep straight. No more children to pretend to be with.

They had run out of time.

Three black SUVs crept down the block like sharks in shallow water. No lights. No sound. Just federal agents with a mission. Federal law enforcement agents, local law enforcement, and a plainclothes officer with cold eyes and a silent badge that read "Dawson."

Officer Dawson stood outside the second vehicle, calm but coiled. He wasn't here just for justice; he was here for the truth. But not yet. Not today.

6:08 a.m. Operation Greenlit

The battering ram knocked on the door in one strike. CRACK.

"FEDERAL AGENTS! HANDS IN THE AIR, NOW!"

Andrés jolted from the couch, heart pounding. "Emma…"

Emma screamed. "Ben?!"

Tactical agents swarmed the room, weapons trained.

"GET DOWN! FACE DOWN!"

Andrés complied, dropping to his knees. "Please! My wife, she's not well…"

But Emma stood frozen, eyes wild, clutching the yellow blanket.

"You're not taking him!" she shouted. "BEN, RUN!"

Her gaze darted toward the kitchen knife block.

"DON'T MOVE!" an agent barked.

She lunged for the counter.

"TASER! TASER!"

The crackle of electricity tore through the air.

Emma collapsed to the floor with a howl, her body seizing as the yellow blanket slipped from her grasp. She hit the linoleum hard, limbs jerking, her mouth twitching incoherently.

"Subject secured," the lead agent said. "The house is clear."

Andres sat in a heap on the living room rug, his hands cuffed behind his back. "You didn't have to do that," he cried. "She's sick. She didn't mean it."

A federal agent replied, "Tell that to the lives she tore apart."

Emma was loaded into an ambulance under heavy guard, placed on suicide watch, and sedated. She mumbled the whole time, repeating one word:

"Ben... Ben... my Ben..."

Later that morning, at the county detention facility in Florida, Andres sat in the interrogation room, his hands cuffed to the metal table, eyes red, jaw tight. He didn't speak when the door opened. He didn't flinch when the man in the dark gray shirt stepped inside.

Officer Dawson walked in silently, closing the door behind him.

He sat across the table, staring for a long moment before reaching into his folder and pulling out photographs.

One was of Matthew, aged eight, standing with Emma in a staged Christmas photo. Another was Elijah Gonzalez, asleep in a stroller as a young child. The third was a forensic image of the park cliffside, where Elijah had fallen.

Dawson slid them across the table slowly.

Andres swallowed hard. "Is this necessary?"

"Yes."

"You don't know what it was like," Andres said hoarsely. "She couldn't handle it. After Jacob, Carlos… Ben…" He closed his eyes. "She thought God was punishing her."

"She was wrong," Dawson replied flatly.

"She thought she could fix it. She thought if she could just be better, if God gave her one more chance…"

"So, she took Elijah Gonzalez from the mall," Dawson interrupted. "And when he died, she took another child from a police station and convinced herself it was fate."

Andres couldn't look at him. "It was the only way she could survive."

Dawson leaned forward. "And you? What's your excuse?"

Andres didn't answer.

Dawson stared at him. "You'll be charged federally for kidnapping, obstruction, falsifying documents, and identity fraud. Your wife is facing the same. If she's declared incompetent to stand trial, you'll carry the full weight."

Still, Andres said nothing.

Dawson stood, gathering the photos.

"She called for Ben during the takedown," he said coldly. "She still doesn't know the truth. And she probably never will."

He turned to the door. His hand paused on the knob.

For a moment, it looked like he might say something else.

But he didn't.

He walked out.

Back in New York, later that afternoon, Matthew sat on a bench outside the medical building, his phone buzzing quietly in his palm as he waited for his mother.

It was a message from an unknown number that had reached out the day before.

"They're in custody. She went down screaming your name. It's over."

He stared at the screen, his thumb hovering over the reply button. But what was there to say?

He set the phone down and leaned back against the bench, eyes toward the sky. He should have felt relieved. But all he felt was weight. Like the truth was finally out, but the pain it left behind still needed a place to go.

Elena stepped out of the building and walked toward him. "You okay?"

"No," Matthew whispered. "But I think we're closer."

She sat beside him and took his hand. The sun was beginning to rise higher in the sky. For the first time in a long time, it didn't feel suffocating.

It felt like the beginning.

Chapter 34
Unraveled

The steel doors of the Detention Center in New York slammed shut behind the transport officers, echoing down the corridor like a verdict. Emma and Andres Diaz had arrived, flown from Florida to New York under federal custody, shackled hand and foot, their names now tied to two decades of lies, kidnapping, and stolen lives.

Emma hadn't spoken during the flight. She had stared out the window with the yellow prison blanket draped around her shoulders like a security net, humming under her breath. Andres had been equally silent, hands trembling in his lap, lips moving in what might've been prayer or guilt.

The interrogation room was cold. The walls were bare. A camera watched silently from the corner of the ceiling.

Detective Kramer sat across from them, her case file thick with photos, reports, affidavits, and now sworn testimony from Grace Harper and Matthew Colon.

She flipped to the first photo on the table. It was a picture of Elijah Gonzalez, age four, smiling beneath a park swing.

Emma's eyes darted to it and then back to Kramer. "That's Ben," she said softly. "That's my son."

Kramer didn't blink. "That's Elijah Gonzalez. And he wasn't your child."

Emma's fingers were twitching. "He was mine. God gave him back to me. After what He took from me."

Kramer's voice was like ice.

"And then you lost him. And you stole another boy, Matthew Colon. You walked into a police station with forged papers, took him while his real family was falling apart, and kept him for eighteen years."

Emma tilted her head, lips curling into something that wasn't quite a smile. "And? I saved him. He would've been lost just like Ben."

The door banged open. Elena stormed in, fury blazing in her eyes.

"You…" Her voice cracked with rage.

Emma lifted her cuffed hands, flicking them dismissively. "Oh, spare me the tears. Boo-hoo. He's mine. I raised him. Fed him. Loved him. What did you do? Sit around and cry?"

Gasps rippled through the room.

Javier stepped forward, his voice trembling with fury. "You kidnapped our son."

Emma leaned back, her smirk widening. "No. I rescued him. And you can call it whatever you want, but I'll always be the one he remembers when he closes his eyes at night."

Police moved quickly, stepping between them. Javier and Elena strained against their hold, shouting over one another.

Elena's voice was sharp and shaking. "You stole eighteen years of his life!"

Emma's eyes glittered coldly. "Get out and get over it. I have his memories now."

"Close the door," Kramer ordered, jaw tight.

Kramer turned back to Emma. "A home you built on the bones of lies."

From the corner, Andrés flinched like the words had struck him.

Emma looked at him, then back at Kramer. "I didn't do it alone."

Kramer leaned forward. "Go on."

Emma's breathing quickened. "Andres... He helped. He forged the paperwork. He coached me on what to say. He found the fire report and even brought me the clothes to make it look like we were at the apartment building that night."

Andres' eyes widened. "Emma..."

Emma turned to him with desperation. "Tell them! Tell them it was your idea! Tell them you made me do it!"

Kramer remained stone-faced. "Mrs. Diaz, you're under investigation for federal kidnapping, aggravated identity fraud, obstruction of justice, and psychiatric endangerment of a minor. If you're claiming coercion, that is a separate legal defense."

Emma stood up abruptly, yanking against her cuffs. "He manipulated me! He knew I was grieving! He said we could start over..."

Andres slammed his hands on the table, cuffs rattling. "Enough!"

The outburst shocked even the officers standing outside the glass.

Emma froze.

Andres looked up slowly, the cracks in his armor finally showing. His eyes were bloodshot, his voice low and broken.

"She didn't lie. Not entirely."

Kramer flipped a new page in her notebook. "Mr. Diaz, you're waiving your right to remain silent?"

He nodded.

"I knew Ben died in that bathtub," Andres began, voice shaking. "I knew Carlos was barely breathing when we placed him by the trash cans."

Kramer's pen stilled.

Andres looked down. "She was losing her mind. She blamed herself for all of them. She stopped eating. She'd stand outside at night calling for Ben. I didn't know what else to do. So, I... played along. I told her that maybe God would bring Ben back. That maybe... if she were faithful enough, if she kept watching, she'd get a second chance."

"And then Elijah came," Kramer said.

Andres nodded slowly. "She saw him at the mall. Said he had the same eyes. The same mouth. She followed the mother around the mall. I should've stopped her...I should've called the police. But she looked at me like I was the only one who understood. She said we could be a family again."

"And so, you had acknowledged that Emma took him."

"I did."

"And when he went missing that night of the fire...?"

"She broke all over again. I couldn't keep her grounded. She wouldn't sleep. She kept hearing his voice. I thought it was over. I thought she'd finally be committed."

Andres exhaled deeply. "Then the next morning, we went to the police station to make a police report for the boy. And she said, 'It's him.' I told her no. I begged her not to do it. Like she'd been reborn. She looked at me and said, 'See? He found his way home.'"

"And you let her keep him," Kramer said coldly.

"I forged the papers," Andres admitted. "I lied to the police. I moved us from New York to Florida. I did everything she asked."

"Why?"

Andres stared at Emma.

"Because I thought if I just gave her what she wanted... maybe I wouldn't lose her, too."

Emma let out a trembling gasp. "You bastard..."

"You were sick, Emma. I knew it. And I didn't stop you. I told myself I was saving you, but all I did was ruin more lives."

Kramer closed the file.

"That'll be enough for now."

She nodded to the guards.

"Transfer them to federal holding. Emma will be remanded for psychiatric evaluation before any arraignment. Andres... you'll be going in for a full booking."

Emma's scream echoed off the walls as they lifted her from her chair.

"Ben! BEN! Don't let them take me! BEN!"

Andres didn't look at her as they dragged her out. She fought against the cuffs, cursing him, begging, crying, twisting herself into a storm of voices. Andrés sat back down, staring at the blank table in front of him.

He finally looked like a man who knew he was guilty.

Not just in the eyes of the law… but in the eyes of the only child who had ever called him Dad.

Matthew sat alone in a private room reserved for victims and witnesses. The city buzzed just beyond the glass, indifferent to the fact that his entire life had just shifted again.

The door opened, not Kramer, but Javier and Elena.

They stopped in the doorway, faces flushed from the confrontation in the other room.

"We're sorry," Javier said, voice low. "We promised we'd keep it together if we saw them… but we couldn't."

Elena's eyes shimmered. "We lost it, Matthew. I'm so sorry."

Matthew stood, shaking his head. "Don't be. I get it. After everything… I'd be furious too."

For a moment, no one moved. Then Javier squeezed his shoulder.

Then Detective Kramer stepped in, placing a printed transcript in Matthew's hands. It was Andrés Diaz's confession.

Matthew's eyes scanned it, stopping on the lines that stung most:

I did everything she asked… Because I thought if I just gave her what she wanted, maybe I wouldn't lose her, too.

He closed the folder.

Eighteen years he'd waited to hear the truth.

And now that it had arrived, it didn't feel like justice.

It felt like a wound reopened.

Chapter 35
The Ones Who Waited

The soft glow of candles flickered along the steps of the old stone church on the corner. Dozens of people stood gathered in the cool evening air, neighbors, parishioners, friends, community activists, distant relatives, each one clutching a candle, a photo, or a simple handmade sign that read:

"Welcome Home, Matthew."

"The Colon Family Deserves Justice."

"Truth Found. Hope Restored."

Javier stood off to the side of the church steps, his hands deep in his coat pockets, shoulders slightly hunched, not out of shame, but from the heavy ache of all they had carried in silence for so many years. Beside him, Elena clutched a tissue and tried to smile as people approached her, some offering hugs, others just a hand on the shoulder.

The vigil had been organized in less than forty-eight hours. A friend from their old parish had made a few phone calls. Word spread quickly. In a city as fast-paced and jaded as New York, no one expected the kind of turnout they were seeing now.

But here they were.

Because people remembered.

They remembered the missing posters. The nightly news pleas. The years when Elena still passed out flyers long after the reporters stopped caring. The way Javier had stayed quiet, stoic, until his voice was needed for yet another search. They remembered the pain because it never left the block.

And now that Matthew was back, so were they.

He stood near the base of the steps, out of sight, dressed in a plain black coat with the hood up. A few people had recognized him, but no one pushed. They gave him space.

He wasn't ready to be "the story." Not yet.

A local pastor took the mic. "We are here tonight not only to welcome a son home, but to honor the parents who never gave up. And to say out loud what trauma so often silences: you were not forgotten."

Applause rippled gently through the crowd.

Matthew looked over at Elena, who was wiping her eyes again, and Javier, who gave a slight nod to no one in particular.

He wondered what it had cost them to keep hoping. To keep praying. To keep their son's memory alive. To light a candle every year on the day he disappeared.

He wondered if he could ever be as strong as they were.

A young girl, maybe thirteen, approached him, holding a sketchbook. "You're him, right?" she asked softly.

He hesitated. "Yeah."

She flipped the sketchpad around. It was a pencil drawing of him as a child, next to a recent news photo.

"I drew this for you. I wanted to say… I'm glad they found you."

Matthew swallowed. "Thank you."

The girl smiled and backed away quickly, disappearing into the crowd.

It hit him then that this wasn't just his story. It had become something larger, a symbol of what could be restored, even after decades of pain.

The pastor spoke again. "We cannot undo what was taken. However, we can surround this family with the support, love, and strength they need to move forward. The road to healing is long. But they will not walk it alone."

The choir began to hum softly. Candles rose. Heads bowed.

Matthew turned to face his parents.

They didn't say anything.

They didn't have to.

They reached for his hands. And for the first time in years, all three stood together in the open, not lost, not hiding, but found.

Later that night, the three of them sat around the dining room table in their modest home. The candles from the vigil still flickered faintly on the kitchen windowsill.

Elena poured hot tea into mismatched mugs while Javier flipped through a box of old photographs.

"You remember this?" he asked, holding up a picture of Matthew at age three, his curly hair wild, cheeks round, and smile bright.

Matthew looked at it as if he were trying to access another life.

"I don't," he admitted. "But... it feels like I should."

Elena reached over and placed her hand on his.

"You don't have to remember everything to belong here," she said gently. "You're our son. That's the only part that matters."

Matthew nodded slowly.

He turned the photo over. On the back, in Elena's handwriting, It read: Matthew's first church Easter, age 3, he wouldn't stop dancing.

"I want to get that back," Matthew whispered. "Not the memory, but the feeling. Of being whole. Being safe."

"You will," Javier said. "Maybe not all at once. But piece by piece."

There was a long pause.

Then Matthew asked, "Do you think… Emma and Andres, who did this… believed they were doing the right thing?"

Elena and Javier exchanged a look.

Elena answered first. "Delusion can look a lot like devotion when pain is left unchecked."

Javier added, "But believing a lie doesn't make it true. And it doesn't make it right."

Matthew nodded, heart heavy with a truth he wasn't sure he could ever fully hold.

He looked at the clock.

Tomorrow was the arraignment hearing.

Emma and Andres would be standing before a judge for the first time in their lives with their crimes laid bare.

And he would be there.

To hear what they had to say.

To see them stripped of the fantasy.

To witness the cost of silence and the slow undoing of deception.

He stood and stretched.

"Let's get some rest," he said.

And as they each retreated to their rooms, Matthew lingered for a moment by the window.

From the street below, someone had taped a small sign to the lamppost outside:

"Justice is near."

He didn't know who left it.

But somehow, it was precisely what he needed to see.

Chapter 36
The Truth on Record

The courtroom buzzed with nervous tension long before the judge took the bench. Every seat was filled, reporters lined the back wall, sketch artists worked in hurried strokes, and court officers positioned themselves with extra care, prepared for the emotional storm that was sure to follow.

Matthew sat quietly in the second row, sandwiched between Elena and Javier. His hands were clasped tightly in his lap, heart pounding against his ribs. This wasn't just another hearing. This was the hearing, the moment the truth would no longer be whispered behind closed doors but spoken aloud for the world to hear.

On the other side of the room, Emma and Andres Diaz were seated at the defense table, both in matching orange jumpsuits. Andres stared forward, jaw clenched, eyes hollow. Emma looked out of place, her hair disheveled, her eyes darting from person to person like a trapped animal.

Her hands shook slightly as she leaned toward her lawyer and whispered something. Her attorney nodded but kept his distance. The room could feel her instability like static in the air.

The door at the front of the courtroom opened, and a man stepped through, tall, composed, dressed in a dark suit with a gold badge clipped to his belt.

Officer Dawson.

He approached the witness stand with steady steps, but something in his jaw tightened as he passed the defense table. Emma glanced up. Andres blinked and furrowed his brow, as if something about the man's face nagged at him.

Dawson raised his hand, was sworn in, and sat down.

The prosecutor stepped forward. "Please state your name and occupation for the record."

"Officer Dawson. Special Investigations Division."

The prosecutor continued. "Officer Dawson, how are you connected to this case?"

Dawson exhaled once. "I was one of the officers who was assigned to the reopened missing child report filed under the name Matthew Colon. But I'm here today for a different reason."

He turned his gaze directly to Emma and Andres.

"I'm your son, Carlos."

Gasps echoed through the room. Elena's hand flew to her mouth. Reporters leaned forward, their pens suddenly scribbling furiously. Emma froze, her eyes wide and unblinking. Andres paled.

Carlos continued, voice steady but cracking beneath the surface.

"I am Carlos Diaz, the child who fell from the banister. The child you told the world was dead. I survived. You didn't call for help. You didn't even check if I was breathing. You carried me outside... and left me near the trash cans."

Emma shook her head slowly. "No... no, that's not true..."

"It is," Carlos snapped, years of buried rage flooding through. "You didn't take me to a hospital. You didn't cradle me. You didn't scream for help. You went back upstairs to check on Ben. And when you found him dead... You never looked back."

214

Tears streamed down his face now, but he didn't stop.

"I grew up with a woman named Ms. Shirley."

Carlos motioned toward the witness's gallery.

From the far side of the room, a small woman stood slowly. Gray hair pulled neatly into a bun, dressed in simple church clothes. Ms. Shirley.

The prosecutor turned. "Your Honor, with the court's permission, we'd like to call a surprise witness. Ms. Shirley Dawson."

The judge looked to the defense.

Emma's attorney objected, "This witness was not disclosed—"

"She's a direct eyewitness to the survival of the Diaz child," the prosecutor argued. "Her testimony is critical to the veracity of the charges."

The judge nodded. "I'll allow it."

Ms. Shirley was sworn in and gently helped to the stand. She glanced at Carlos with soft eyes before facing the courtroom.

"I lived next door to the Diazes in New Jersey," she began. "That afternoon, I heard a scream earlier in the day. I continued with my day. I went to the grocery store and, on my way back home later that evening, while taking out the trash, I saw Carlos. He was lying near the side of the house, by the trash cans. He was bruised, bleeding, and barely breathing. I didn't see anyone else. I scooped him up and drove him straight to the local hospital, then I nursed him at home."

"Why didn't you tell the family?"

"I left a note. I was angry. Furious. I told them the boy was alive, and he was next door at my house, but no one came for him. No one. Days turned to weeks, then to months. Then I filed for guardianship."

Her voice cracked. "I raised him as my own."

Carlos sat trembling, jaw clenched, hands gripping the witness box.

"I always wondered why," he whispered. "Why didn't you look for me? Why Ben was the only one you cried for."

Emma shot to her feet. "That's a lie!" she shouted. "That's not my son! My Carlos died! He...he was taken from me! You're just trying to confuse me!"

"You could've had me," Carlos said, voice low but sharp. "You could've had a real family. Instead, you built a fantasy around a dead child and forgot the living one."

Emma lunged forward, her screams cracking through the air. Bailiffs swarmed in as she thrashed against their grip.

"BEN! BEN! NOT HIM! HE'S NOT MINE!"

The judge banged the gavel. "Order! Order in this courtroom!"

Andres looked at Carlos, tears finally falling. "I knew," he said, voice hollow. "I knew you looked familiar. But I couldn't believe it."

"You didn't want to believe it," Carlos replied. "Because then you'd have to face what you did."

The judge motioned for the courtroom to be cleared. Reporters were escorted out. A recess was called.

But the damage had already been done.

Outside the courtroom, Matthew stood frozen.

He had come face-to-face with his captors.

Instead, he met a friend.

Carlos approached him, eyes still red, breath shallow.

"I didn't know about you," he said quietly. "Not until recently. But I saw the file… and I saw myself in your story."

Matthew's voice was low. "I can't believe they just left you to die."

They didn't hug. They didn't cry.

They stood together, their shadows stretching across the courthouse floor, two strangers bound by the same wound. Somewhere behind them, the muffled echoes of Emma's screams still clung to the air.

Matthew looked at Carlos, his voice barely above a whisper. "This isn't the end."

Carlos nodded.

And for now, that was enough.

Chapter 37
I'm Not Him

The trial stretched into its third week, each day tightening the invisible cord between the prosecution's table and the defense. Witness after witness stepped into the light of the stand, Elena, voice trembling as she recounted the night her son disappeared; Javier, jaw clenched as he pointed to the defendants without hesitation; Matthew, answering each question with a steady calm that belied the storm inside him.

Detective Kramer's testimony hit like a hammer. She walked the jury through the DNA evidence, the forged documents, and the citywide cold case initiative that finally brought the truth to light. Then came the photographs, faded prints of a little boy in a yellow blanket, police reports yellowed with time, the autopsy that proved Ben Diaz's tragic death.

The defense tried to spin a different story. Emma's attorney painted her as a savior, a woman who had "rescued" a boy from a life of uncertainty. Andres's lawyer called him a man trapped by loyalty and fear. But with each argument, the prosecution countered with hard, unshakable facts.

By the time closing arguments were finished, the air in the courtroom had grown heavier. Every eye followed the jury as they filed out to deliberate, the sound of the door closing behind them echoing like the toll of a bell.

Hours later, the bailiff's voice rang out.

"Jury's back!"

The door to the jury room swung open. Twelve men and women filed back into their seats, faces unreadable, eyes forward. The hum of the courtroom stilled to a breathless pause.

The judge leaned forward, resting his hands on the bench. His voice carried the weight of the moment.

"Ladies and gentlemen of the jury," he said evenly, "have you reached a verdict?"

"Guilty, all counts."

Carlos had not moved; his shadows stretched across the polished floor, bound by a silence thicker than words.

The words rang through the courtroom like a crack of thunder.

Gasps echoed. Some people wept. Reporters scrambled for their notepads. Flashbulbs from sketch artists' pens flew across parchment. One woman in the back faintly whispered, "Thank God."

At the prosecution table, the assistant district attorney exhaled deeply.

Matthew sat still. Frozen. Hands gripping the bench in front of him, jaw clenched.

Beside him, Elena broke down in tears. Javier reached over and held her hand, the tremor in his fingers betraying the storm inside.

Across the room, Andres Diaz buckled.

He didn't faint. He didn't scream. He folded forward in his seat, shaking. His shoulders trembled as the bailiffs stepped toward him. His face crumpled. Then he began to sob.

Loud, raw, unguarded.

"I just wanted to fix it…" he whispered. "I just wanted her to smile again…"

Emma turned to him sharply. Her face twisted, not in grief, but in disgust.

"Don't cry now," she hissed. "You were always weak."

She stood abruptly, her shackled hands raising as if in performance. Her voice changed, trembled, cracked, turned high-pitched and wild.

"No, no, no," she wailed. "They tricked you! I didn't do this! I was sick! He…he made me! Andres told me to take them! I was only trying to be a mother again!"

She dropped to her knees dramatically in front of the jury box.

"I loved them. I gave them a home! They needed me! You don't understand what it's like to lose a child!"

The bailiffs stepped in, but she lashed out with her arms.

Then she turned toward Matthew.

Her eyes locked on him with such force that it chilled the entire row behind him.

"Ben!" she cried out, voice shrill and shaking. "Ben! Tell them! Tell them I was your mother!"

Matthew stood slowly.

He was calmer than he had been in weeks.

"I'm not him," he said clearly.

Emma's eyes widened.

"I'm not Ben. I'm Matthew Colon."

Gasps filled the room again. The judge pounded the gavel.

Emma screamed.

"No! NO! Don't say that! You're mine! You were mine! Don't do this, please...Ben! BEN!"

She lunged forward, but the bailiffs restrained her. Her body hit the floor hard, kicking, flailing.

"Come back, Ben! Come back! Don't leave me again!"

She was dragged from the courtroom, heels scraping across the floor, tears pouring down her face, still screaming.

"BEN! DON'T LEAVE ME!"

Matthew turned away and walked out slowly with Elena and Javier beside him, heads held high.

He never looked back.

As the doors slammed shut behind Matthew, Emma was dragged into the holding corridor, where she pounded on the two-way mirror that lined the hallway.

She stared at her reflection and the shadowy figures on the other side.

Her fists slammed again and again, bruising.

"Come back, Ben!" she sobbed, head pressed to the glass. "I'm sorry! I'll be better! I'll be good! Just come back..."

Then, she turned.

And her eyes met the one man standing just feet away.

Carlos.

She blinked, as if only now recognizing him from the witness stand.

"You," she whispered. "You."

Her voice turned sharp. Cold. Spiteful.

"If you hadn't fallen off that damn banister, none of this would've happened.

Carlos didn't respond.

Emma's face was contorted. "You were always too wild. You ran. You climbed. You broke everything. If you hadn't fallen, I would've finished the bath. Ben would still be alive."

Tears welled in Carlos's eyes.

"You're the reason this happened!" she screamed. "It's your fault! You ruined everything!"

Bailiffs dragged her away as she cursed him, sobbed, pleaded, laughed, and screamed all at once, completely untethered from reality.

Carlos stood there, unmoving.

Until he felt a hand on his shoulder.

Ms. Shirley.

She was behind him now, eyes glossy, expression full of love.

She wrapped her arms around him from behind and said gently, "That's not your fault, baby. It never was."

Another officer stepped forward, resting a hand on Carlos's back.

"You did your job. You told the truth."

Carlos nodded, but his face was crumbling. Years of repressed memories cracked under the pressure of those final words. All he ever wanted was to be seen and loved by his parents. But instead, his mother had blamed him for the death of his brother.

A child she hadn't let go of.

And a child she'd forgotten she already had.

Carlos turned to Ms. Shirley and wrapped his arms around her, burying his face in her shoulder as the courtroom behind him quieted, and Emma's screams faded down the hallway.

For the first time since he was a boy, Carlos wept not just for what he lost...

...but for what he survived.

Chapter 38
The Healing Place

The night after the trial, the city outside Ms. Shirley's small apartment hummed as usual, sirens in the distance, taxis rushing by, a dog barking somewhere off in the dark. But inside, all was still.

Carlos sat on her worn brown couch, his face dimly lit by the soft glow of a reading lamp. His elbows were on his knees, his hands covering his mouth. He hadn't spoken in over twenty minutes.

Ms. Shirley moved slowly, the way older women of wisdom do, without rush or fear. She placed a cup of peppermint tea on the table before him, along with a small cloth-bound Holy Scriptures she had carried for over forty years. It was weathered, its corners soft, the gold leaf on the pages long faded.

She sat across from him, her spine straight but her eyes gentle.

"I know that look, son," she said. "That's the look of someone carryin' what he was never meant to carry."

Carlos exhaled shakily. "She said it was my fault. That if I hadn't fallen... Ben would still be alive."

Ms. Shirley shook her head slowly. "I heard every word. And I rebuke that lie in the name of the Lord."

Carlos looked at her, tears pressing at the edges of his vision.

She opened the Holy Scriptures and turned a few pages. Her finger landed gently on the verse.

"The LORD is nigh unto them that are of a broken heart; and saveth such as be of a contrite spirit."

Psalm 34:18 KJV.

Her voice was calm, low, and steady.

"You were just a child, Carlos. You were five years old. You didn't break your family. The devil did that with confusion and deception. But you? You survived. And that's no accident."

Carlos dropped his head into his hands. "Why didn't they want me?"

Ms. Shirley rose and sat beside him. Her hand pressed gently against his back.

"They were broken people trying to make themselves whole with broken choices. But just because they lost their way doesn't mean you were lost. God never let go of you, not once."

She turned the page again.

"When my father and my mother forsake me, then the LORD will take me up."

Psalm 27:10 KJV.

Carlos choked on a sob. Ms. Shirley reached out and pulled him into her arms.

"I've been waiting years for this day, baby. Not the courtroom, not the verdict. This moment right here. You, understanding who you are."

She leaned back and cupped his face in her hands.

"You are not what they left behind. You are not what they forgot. You are not what she said in anger. You are a child of the Most High God, and He didn't forget you."

Carlos nodded, but his face was full of anguish.

"She wanted Ben so bad... She just erased me."

"She tried," Ms. Shirley said. "But God preserved you. You fell, but you were caught. You were abandoned, but you were rescued. Man forgot you, but never by your Maker."

She opened her Holy Scriptures again, tears gently sliding down her face now, too.

"Before I formed thee in the belly I knew thee; and before thou camest forth out of the womb I sanctified thee..."

Jeremiah 1:5 KJV.

Carlos whispered, "I don't know how to heal from this."

Ms. Shirley smiled gently. "Healing doesn't start with knowing. It starts with surrender. You don't have to know everything. You have to let God do what only He can."

She slid the Holy Scriptures into his lap. "Start here. Every time you hear her voice telling you it was your fault, open this book. Let His voice be louder than hers."

Carlos held the Holy Scriptures to his chest and closed his eyes.

Later that night, after he had fallen asleep on the couch, Ms. Shirley stood quietly in the doorway, watching the boy she'd once cradled in a hospital waiting room, half dead and without a name, now finally sleeping with peace on his face.

She whispered a prayer over him.

"Lord, you spared this boy for a reason. You brought him through the fire and the flood. Now bring him into a place of rest. Cover his mind. Heal his heart. Let him walk in truth, not in trauma. In Jesus' name. Amen."

She turned back toward her room, pausing just once to glance at the flickering streetlight outside the window.

It swayed in the wind.

And she felt it again, the unmistakable peace of the Holy Ghost…settling over her home like a warm blanket.

She whispered to herself, smiling through tears.

"He restoreth my soul."

Psalm 23:3 KJV.

Chapter 39
Beauty for Ashes

The cemetery was quiet except for the soft crunch of gravel beneath their feet and the whispering wind that stirred the leaves overhead. The late afternoon sun hung low in the sky, casting golden light over rows of headstones like Heaven was touching earth just enough to remind the living they weren't alone.

Matthew strolled, hands in his coat pockets, unsure if he was ready for this moment, uncertain if anyone ever could be.

Beside him, Carlos walked in silence, his gaze set ahead, the weight of something unseen pressing heavily on his shoulders. They hadn't said much on the drive. There was now an understanding between them, a brotherhood forged not in childhood, but in pain.

At the far end of the cemetery, beneath a willow tree, Carlos stopped.

"This is it."

Matthew looked down at the small gravestone in front of them. It was plain. Humble. The lettering was carved with care.

Benjamin Isaiah Diaz

1991 – 1995

"You are loved."

Carlos knelt beside it and brushed away a few fallen leaves.

"I discovered he was my brother after being assigned to the Special Investigations Division," he said quietly.

Matthew stood still, watching him.

Carlos' voice grew thick. He placed a small photo face down, one he had kept since the day they identified the body."

"I was looking through the case file and saw the house. I had to go back to see for myself. The house was deserted. He stood slowly, staring at the headstone like it held a piece of him, too."

"I started looking through the closets. Upstairs, I found a box hidden behind some blankets. Inside was a picture, an old one. Of Ben. And Me."

Carlos swallowed hard. "And Jacob."

Matthew blinked, stunned.

"That's when I knew," Carlos whispered. "They were my parents, too. Emma and Andres. They left me by the trash cans when I was five years old. Thought I died. But Ms. Shirley found me."

Silence fell between them again, heavy, heartbreaking, and honest.

"They left me," Carlos added, his voice trembling. "But somehow… I made it, I survived."

Matthew nodded, eyes stinging. "We did."

Together, they stood side by side at Ben's grave, two boys once lost, finally facing the truth that had bound them, broken them, and brought them home.

He swallowed hard.

He looked up at Matthew. "I didn't tell Emma and Andres at the trial. They didn't deserve to know what had happened to me or how I had grown up. They left both of us. Me, in the dirt and Ben in the dark."

Matthew crouched beside him. "And yet you gave Ben something they never gave us."

Carlos nodded slowly. "A place to rest."

For a moment, they sat in silence, two men who barely knew each other and were beginning to develop a friendship. The branches above swayed gently, as if covering them in a gentle grace.

Then Carlos whispered, "You know... I always blamed myself."

Matthew looked at him.

"I thought if I hadn't fallen... if I hadn't distracted her... maybe Ben would've lived. Maybe she wouldn't have lost her mind. Maybe none of this would've happened."

Matthew placed a hand on his shoulder. "She wanted to believe what she wanted. No matter what."

Carlos stared at the headstone. "I think... we were both sacrificed on her altar of grief."

Matthew said nothing. The truth didn't need repeating. It just needed a place to rest.

After several minutes, the sound of soft footsteps caught their attention.

They turned.

A couple approached slowly, arm in arm. The woman held a bouquet of white lilies. The man's eyes met theirs with somber recognition.

It was the Gonzalez family.

Carlos stood. Matthew followed, heart quickening.

Mr. Gonzalez gave a respectful nod. "Are you two here for Ben Diaz?"

Carlos nodded. "Yes, sir."

The woman spoke softly. "We came to visit our son. Elijah."

Carlos's eyes widened. "He's buried here?"

She pointed gently. "Just across the path."

They walked together in silence to a small headstone etched with a smiling angel.

Elijah Mateo Gonzalez

Forever Loved. Never Forgotten

1990 – 1995

"Though he were dead, yet shall he live" – John 11:25 KJV.

Mrs. Gonzalez knelt and laid the flowers. She kissed two fingers and pressed them to the top of the stone. Mr. Gonzalez looked at Carlos and Matthew, his voice thick with emotion.

"He loved superheroes. He wanted to be one. Said God gave him powers in his dreams."

Carlos smiled faintly. "He was one."

Matthew stepped forward slowly.

"I know… it can never be enough. But I am sorry. For what my captors did. For the lies. For your loss. For everything."

Carlos added, "We were victims, too. But we still wanted to come. To say… we mourn with you."

Mrs. Gonzalez turned, her eyes brimming with tears. "It's not your fault."

Mr. Gonzalez nodded. "You were just children. You didn't choose this."

He reached into his jacket and pulled out a worn copy of the Holy Scriptures. "We've been walking through this valley for years. And the only thing that carried us was this."

He opened to Isaiah 61:3 KJV.

"To appoint unto them that mourn in Zion, to give unto them beauty for ashes, the oil of joy for mourning, the garment of praise for the spirit of heaviness…"

He paused, looking at Elijah's grave, then at the two young men beside him.

"…that they might be called trees of righteousness, the planting of the LORD, that he might be glorified."

Carlos closed his eyes.

Matthew whispered, "I don't want their legacy to end with what they did. I want ours to begin with what we do now."

Mrs. Gonzalez nodded. "Then you've already started."

She reached out and embraced Matthew, then Carlos. Mr. Gonzalez followed.

And for a moment, under the long shadows of sunset, sorrow and redemption shared the same breath.

As the Gonzalez family left, Carlos and Matthew lingered between the two graves, Ben's and Elijah's.

Matthew pulled out his own Holy Scriptures, which Elena had given him just days earlier. He turned slowly, then began to read aloud.

"The LORD is my shepherd; I shall not want.

He maketh me to lie down in green pastures: he leadeth me beside the still waters.

He restoreth my soul: he leadeth me in the paths of righteousness for his name's sake."

Psalm 23:1-3 KJV

Carlos listened, eyes closed.

Matthew continued.

"Yea, though I walk through the valley of the shadow of death, I will fear no evil: for thou art with me..."

His voice cracked

"...thy rod and thy staff they comfort me.

He looked at Carlos.

"We survived the valley."

Carlos nodded. "Now we rise."

They placed small stones at the foot of both graves, symbols of remembrance, promises never to forget. As they turned to leave, the wind swept through the trees, and for a fleeting moment, it felt like the past had finally been laid to rest.

Not erased.

Not forgotten.

But redeemed.

Chapter 40
The Table of Restoration

The house was quiet, but it wasn't the hollow quiet of grief anymore. It was the soft quiet of a home that had started to breathe again. Sunlight poured through the kitchen window, spilling onto the table where Elena stood pressing napkins with careful fingers.

Javier leaned against the counter, arms folded, watching her.

"You've redone that one three times," he said gently.

She looked up, eyes wet with both nerves and hope. "I want everything to be perfect."

He walked over and took her hands in his. "They're not coming for the napkin folds. They're coming because they're part of this now."

Elena exhaled deeply. "It still feels like a dream. Like at any moment, it could all… vanish again."

"It won't."

She smiled faintly. "You sound so sure."

"I am." He squeezed her hands. "Because God said He would restore what the locusts had eaten. And I believe He's doing that."

She nodded slowly.

"And I will restore to you the years that the locust hath eaten…"

Joel 2:25, KJV

That afternoon, Matthew returned from the gravesite with Carlos by his side. They didn't speak much at first, just passed through the door with the weight of something sacred hanging over them. Their eyes were red, their spirits heavy, but something in their posture had shifted.

They looked like brothers.

Real ones.

Elena had felt it in her chest the moment they walked in. A kind of stillness that said: This is what it means to begin again.

She invited him back for dinner on Sunday. A simple Sunday meal. Nothing elaborate, nothing loud. Just food, candles, a table, and people who had survived the same storm.

Carlos had hesitated when invited. So had Ms. Shirley. But Matthew had placed a hand on his shoulder and said, "Come back."

And he had.

Now the table was set. The roast was in the oven. Elena had made arroz con gandules, fried sweet plantains, and her mother's old coconut cake recipe. She wanted the meal to feel familiar, even if the family gathered around it was newly stitched together.

The doorbell rang.

Elena wiped her hands on a towel. Javier opened the door.

Carlos stood there in a button-down shirt, hands tucked in his pockets, a nervous smile pulling at the corners of his mouth.

Ms. Shirley stood beside him, a warm casserole dish in her hands, her Holy Scriptures tucked under one arm.

"I brought baked macaroni," she said. "And a whole lotta gratitude."

Elena laughed and stepped forward to hug her. "You didn't have to bring anything."

"I didn't come empty-handed to the house where God just performed a miracle," Ms. Shirley said. "This table is holy ground tonight."

Carlos stepped inside slowly, eyes scanning the family photos along the wall. There was a baby Matthew in Javier's arms, one of Elena's, holding a tiny hand in a hospital blanket.

He swallowed. "You never stopped believing."

"No," Javier said. "Never."

Elena stepped beside him. "There was always a seat at our table. Even when we didn't know your name yet."

Carlos blinked, eyes glossy.

Matthew appeared in the hallway and smiled. "You guys made it."

Carlos gave a shy nod. "We did."

The meal was humble, but sacred.

They laughed softly at stories from Matthew's early years. Javier shared a story about trying to build a treehouse, only to end up hammering a nail into a water pipe. Ms. Shirley shared that Carlos once convinced a neighbor's cat to ride in a bicycle basket, like a creature in a costume.

Carlos was quiet at first, but slowly, the weight he carried began to loosen. He let himself smile. He let himself eat. He let himself listen as Elena said grace and thanked God not just for food, but for healing.

"Lord, You said in Your Word that Thou preparest a table before me in the presence of mine enemies. And Lord, You have done even better. You prepared a table in the presence of redemption. Of mercy. Of family. Let every bite we eat tonight remind us that You are a restorer. A healer. A Father to the fatherless. In Jesus' name. Amen."

Psalm 23:5, KJV

They all echoed a quiet "Amen."

Later that evening, after dinner had been cleared and the sun had long set, Javier lit candles and poured coffee for everyone.

Ms. Shirley and Elena sat on the couch, flipping through a photo album, their laughter warming the room. Matthew leaned against the doorframe of the kitchen, quietly watching his parents with new eyes.

Carlos stood alone by the window, looking out at the street.

Javier stepped beside him. "You okay?"

Carlos nodded. "It's just strange. I've spent most of my life wondering what it would feel like to belong. And now that I do… I'm afraid I'll lose it."

Javier put a hand on his shoulder.

"We don't lose what God restores. We keep it."

Carlos looked at him, surprised by the certainty in his voice.

Javier smiled. "I learned a long time ago that families don't always come in straight lines. Sometimes they come through pain. Through grace. Through strangers who show up and never leave."

Carlos blinked. "Thank you. For this. For tonight."

Javier's voice grew softer. "You're not a guest here, Carlos. You're home."

Before they left, Ms. Shirley stood and held her Holy Scriptures in both hands.

"I know I'm not your blood," she said, looking at Elena and Javier. "But I raised that boy from a hospital bed to a grown man. I've done my best to give him roots.

Elena walked over and hugged her tightly. "You're as much family as anyone in this house."

Ms. Shirley whispered, "To God be the glory."

Carlos stood at the threshold, unsure whether to say goodbye or goodnight.

Matthew walked up beside him.

"You don't have to rush this," he said. "You're not going anywhere. You're part of us now."

Carlos nodded slowly. "I've never had that before."

Matthew smiled. "Me neither. Until now."

Elena handed Carlos a container of leftovers. "For tomorrow. So, you remember this wasn't just one night."

He smiled and blinked back tears. "Thank you."

As he stepped outside with Ms. Shirley, Carlos turned back to look at the house, warm light spilling through the window, laughter still echoing from inside.

He whispered under his breath.

"Behold, how good and how pleasant it is for brethren to dwell together in unity."

Psalm 133:1, KJV

Chapter 41
The Voice of the Found

The community center in New York hadn't seen such a turnout in years. Folding chairs lined the gymnasium floor, shoulder to shoulder, filled with families, social workers, law enforcement officers, church members, teachers, and former foster youth. A large banner hung behind the podium:

"Hope Restored: Awareness for the Missing, the Taken, and the Found"

Elena and Javier sat in the second row, flanked by Ms. Shirley and several volunteers from their local church. A slideshow played in the background, featuring the faces of real missing children, both those found and those still missing. For many, this wasn't just a talk.

It was a homecoming.

At the front of the room stood two friends, bound together by lies, but now standing side by side.

Carlos adjusted the mic.

He looked out over the crowd and took a steadying breath.

"Good evening. My name is Officer Carlos Dawson. And for most of my life, I didn't know who I was."

A hush fell across the room.

"I was left outside as a child, unconscious, after a fall that my parents didn't bother to call in. They assumed I wouldn't make it. I did. I survived."

He paused. His voice cracked slightly, but he didn't break.

"A neighbor named Ms. Shirley found me. She took me to the hospital. She raised me. I avoided the system, built a life, became a police officer, but inside, I never stopped wondering why I wasn't enough for the people who gave me life."

His gaze lifted.

"And then, one day, I found a brother."

A few gasps echoed in the back.

"Not through DNA. Not through some miracle reunion. I found him because a lie had also taken hold of him. Through someone else's grief. He was renamed, reshaped, and raised by the same hands that once left me behind."

He looked at Matthew.

"I thought our story was about being forgotten. But I was wrong."

He turned back to the crowd.

"Our story is about being found. Not just by each other, but by God. Because even when we didn't know who we were, He did."

He opened his Holy Scriptures and read gently:

"Fear thou not; for I am with thee: be not dismayed; for I am thy God:

I will strengthen thee; yea, I will help thee; yea, I will uphold thee

With the right hand of my righteousness."

Isaiah 41:10, KJV

Carlos nodded once, his voice steady.

"We are not here to shame our past. We are here to reclaim it. And to remind every parent, every worker, every stranger in this room: one act of attention can save a child's life. One person's care can rewrite their future."

He stepped back.

Matthew moved forward.

He took the mic and looked out at the faces.

His voice was soft at first.

"My name is Matthew Colon. I spent most of my life thinking I was someone else. Someone named Ben, but I'm Not Him. I was taken as a toddler during a fire, claimed by a woman who said I was hers. She gave me her last name. Her home. Her version of the truth."

He paused.

"But I never felt... whole. I never felt like the pieces fit. And I didn't understand why until I saw my face on a missing child's website. Until the lies began to unravel. And then, everything inside me broke."

He swallowed.

"And then... God started putting it back together."

He turned to Carlos. "He gave me a brother."

He looked toward Elena and Javier. "He gave me my real parents."

He turned to the crowd again. "And He gave me a name. My name."

"But now thus saith the LORD that created thee, O Jacob, and he that formed thee, O Israel,

Fear not: for I have redeemed thee, I have called thee by thy name; thou art mine."

Isaiah 43:1, KJV

Tears shimmered in his eyes.

"I am not who they said I was. I am who God says I am. And to every child still waiting, still lost, still afraid, there is still hope. I found mine. And I will spend the rest of my life helping others find theirs."

The room erupted into applause. Not polite. Not rehearsed.

Honest. Loud. Tearful. Healing.

Some people stood. Others bowed their heads and wept. A few embraced one another silently.

Elena pressed her hand over her heart.

Javier wiped his eyes with the edge of his sleeve.

Ms. Shirley whispered under her breath, "Thank you, Jesus."

The center's director stepped to the front and invited Matthew and Carlos to join a panel of child advocates, investigators, and survivors. But as they walked offstage, something sacred had already happened.

They had changed the air in the room.

Not by being perfect.

But by being whole.

That night, as the center emptied, a young woman approached them, no older than eighteen, her hands trembling and her eyes tired. "My sister disappeared when we were kids," she said. "No one believed me. They said she just ran away."

Carlos and Matthew listened quietly.

She looked down. "But tonight, hearing you… I believe maybe someone will find her. Maybe I will."

Matthew placed a hand on her shoulder. "Don't give up."

Carlos added, "God knows where she is."

She nodded, lips quivering. "Thank you."

Outside, under the city's flickering streetlamps, Carlos and Matthew stood in the cool air, side by side.

Carlos broke the silence. "You think we'll ever be normal?"

Matthew smiled faintly. "I don't think God's calling us to be normal. I think He's calling us to be whole."

Carlos nodded.

Then he looked up at the stars just barely visible through the glow of New York City lights.

"And ye shall know the truth, and the truth shall make you free."

John 8:32, KJV

And for the first time in their lives, they both believed it.

Epilogue
Full Circle

Part I – Elena's Journal Entry

Dear Matthew,

I never stopped believing.

Even when the years felt like centuries. Even when my arms ached for the child I couldn't hold. Even when the world told me to move on, I kept one hand on the door just in case you came home.

Now, every time I see your face, I thank God for mercy I didn't deserve. You've grown into a man of compassion, wisdom, and faith. And though we lost time, I believe with all my heart that God is restoring everything that was stolen.

You are not broken. You are not forgotten. You are not a mistake. You are ours.

Welcome home, son.

Love always,

Mom

As the ink on Elena's final word dried, somewhere miles away, another kind of goodbye was unfolding…

Part II – Carlos at the Cemetery

Carlos knelt in front of a small, marked gravestone nestled beneath a maple tree.

He had returned alone.

The grass was overgrown, and though the marker wasn't yet weathered, Carlos laid fresh lilies at its base. His hand brushed the cold stone, and he exhaled slowly.

"Hey, Ben," he whispered.

The wind answered softly, like a breath through the trees.

"I know I couldn't save you. I was just a kid, too scared and confused. I didn't even know what to do when I found you. But I couldn't let them toss you out like you didn't matter. So, I did what I could; I gave you this place."

He placed a small wooden cross in the ground beside the lilies.

"I came to say goodbye… and to tell you that I forgive them. I'm trying, anyway. For my peace. For yours."

Opening his Holy Scriptures, he read from Isaiah 61:3:

To appoint unto them that mourn in Zion, to give unto them beauty for ashes, the oil of joy for mourning, the garment of praise for the spirit of heaviness…

Tears filled his eyes. "We lost everything, didn't we? But maybe this…" he looked around, "maybe this is where something new can grow."

He stood up, took one last glance at the stone, and whispered, "Rest easy, little brother."

Later that same afternoon, in a different corner of the city, another set of footsteps retraced the path of a life interrupted…

Part III – Matthew at Willow Brook

Matthew stood in an empty parking lot where the Willow Brook used to be, staring at the cracked sidewalk where he had once ridden his red Truck with big wheels.

The space looked bigger now.

The parking lot, once a racetrack in his four-year-old mind, was just concrete and faded paint. But the memories lingered…birthday cake, laughter, a warm voice calling his name.

This was where the story broke.

But also… where it began.

From his pocket, he pulled a folded piece of paper, his restored birth certificate, bearing the name Matthew Elias Colon.

He smiled through the ache.

As he turned to leave, the clouds parted slightly, and a shaft of golden light touched the rooftop.

It wasn't just nostalgia. It was resurrection.

At his car, he whispered, "I'm not him… I'm Matthew Colon."

And for the first time in eighteen years, he felt completely whole.

One year later, the ache of the past had given way to something new, something alive, gathered around a table that was finally full…

Part IV – One Year Later: A Table Made Whole

The Colon family's backyard was filled with laughter, sunlight, and the scent of grilled food. A long wooden table sat beneath glowing string lights, surrounded by family, neighbors, and friends. Children raced through the yard while a gospel playlist blended with the hum of summer.

Javier operated the grill, flipping burgers, while Elena set out plates of rice, beans, and roasted corn. Joy softened her every movement.

Matthew sat beside Carlos at the table, sipping sweet tea as they watched the younger kids run circles around Ms. Shirley, who was pretending to chase them with a kitchen towel.

"You know," Carlos said with a smirk, "I still have trouble calling you brother out loud."

Matthew grinned. "I know. But it fits."

Carlos nodded slowly. "Yeah. It does."

Elena lifted a mason jar of lemonade. "To healing. To answer prayers. And to family."

Everyone clinked glasses.

From her lawn chair, Ms. Shirley called out, "And to God's grace, and to Grace, who told the truth at just the right time!"

Laughter rippled through the yard as Grace, now seeking her doctoral in child psychology, waved shyly from her seat beside Elena.

Javier's voice carried over the noise. "For a long time, this table had an empty seat. But now... It's full. Not just with food, or faces, but with faith. And hope."

Carlos added, "And a future."

The sun dipped behind the trees, casting a golden glow over faces once marked by loss but now lit with restoration. Fireflies began to blink in the dusk.

Matthew leaned back, letting the sound of laughter wash over him like a song.

This was what healing looked like.

This was what coming home felt like.

This was wholeness.

For the first time in decades, the family was not just surviving…they were healing.

And they were doing it together.

The End.

Acknowledgments

First and foremost, I thank God for His grace, guidance, and mercy throughout this journey. This book would not exist without his strength that carried me through the storms.

To my family, thank you for your unconditional love, patience, and support. Every late night, every page rewritten, every emotional scene… You stood by me. Your encouragement gave me the courage to tell this story with honesty and heart.

To every reader who has experienced grief, identity loss, or brokenness, may it remind you that healing is possible, faith is powerful, and truth will always find its way to the light.

To the survivors, the seekers, the ones still holding on, never stop believing that redemption is real.

With gratitude,

Kimberly Cummings

Resources

If you or someone you know has experienced child abduction, abuse, or trauma, the following organizations can provide support, information, and assistance:

National Center for Missing & Exploited Children (NCMEC)

Website: https://www.missingkids.org

24-Hour Hotline: 1-800-843-5678 (1-800-THE-LOST)

National Child Abuse Hotline

Website: https://www.childhelp.org

24-Hour Hotline: 1-800-422-4453 (1-800-4-A-CHILD)

RAINN – Rape, Abuse & Incest National Network

Website: https://www.rainn.org

National Sexual Assault Hotline: 1-800-656-4673

National Runaway Safeline

Website: https://www.1800runaway.org

24-Hour Hotline: 1-800-786-2929 (1-800-RUNAWAY)

Child Find of America

Website: https://www.childfindofamerica.org

Helpline: 1-800-426-5678

For informational purposes only. See full disclaimer at the front of this book.

About the Author

Kimberly Cummings is a powerful storyteller, educator, and advocate with a heart rooted in faith, justice, and healing. With a background in criminal justice and a lifelong commitment to community empowerment, Kimberly writes stories that speak to the soul, exploring identity, loss, resilience, and redemption.

She is the author of several transformative works, including:

A Different Echo: Tiny Words

Walking on the Sea Sand

Cracked Glass Trilogy

She is also the creator of a growing collection of inspirational personal journals designed to support healing, reflection, and wellness.

Her upcoming release, Through the Storms: A Journey of Faith, Hope, and Perseverance, continues her mission to bring truth, purpose, and emotional healing to the page, a powerful narrative of transformation and faith.

When she's not writing, Kimberly leads a training school, uplifts young people through education, and continues to serve her community with compassion and purpose. She believes in the power of second chances, the unbreakable bond of family, and the unwavering grace of God.

To learn more about her books and journals, visit her Amazon Author Page or connect through her email or website:

Email: scratchpadcreate@gmail.com or www. kimberlycummingsauthor.com